"I Swore I Wouldn't Tonight,"

Alex began thickly. "But you shouldn't look at me like that." He reached out and pulled her to him urgently, his mouth coming down to cover hers hungrily, insistently, as though long deprived of the taste of her. Yielding, Julie responded, her own senses clamoring for fulfillment. He was kissing her desperately and deeply, and Julie reeled with a pleasure so sweet that she was mindless to everything but Alex's passion and the sensations he created so effortlessly. . . .

Dazed, she dragged herself from his arms, trembling all over. She buried her face in her hands. "Get out of here, Alex," she sobbed.

KAREN YOUNG
and her husband, Paul, have moved eighteen times during twenty-five years of marriage. Because of their mobile life-style, Karen has observed many different types of people and has included them in her plots. *Yesterday's Promise* is Karen's first Silhouette Romance.

Dear Reader:

I'd like to take this opportunity to thank you for all your support and encouragement of Silhouette Romances.

Many of you write in regularly, telling us what you like best about Silhouette, which authors are your favorites. This is a tremendous help to us as we strive to publish the best contemporary romances possible.

All the romances from Silhouette Books are for you, so enjoy this book and the many stories to come. I hope you'll continue to share your thoughts with us, and invite you to write to us at the address below:

Karen Solem
Editor-in-Chief
Silhouette Books
P.O. Box 769
New York, N.Y. 10019

KAREN YOUNG
Yesterday's Promise

Silhouette *Romance*

Published by Silhouette Books New York

America's Publisher of Contemporary Romance

SILHOUETTE BOOKS, a Simon & Schuster Division of
GULF & WESTERN CORPORATION
1230 Avenue of the Americas, New York, N.Y. 10020

Copyright © 1983 by Karen Young

Distributed by Pocket Books

ISBN: 0-671-57212-1

First Silhouette Books printing March, 1983

10 9 8 7 6 5 4 3 2 1

Map by Ray Lundgren

America's Publisher of Contemporary Romance

Printed in the U.S.A.

Yesterday's Promise

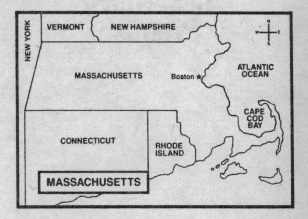

Chapter One

"Julie, do you realize it's almost seven o'clock?" The exasperated voice of Ann Lawson, friend and apartment neighbor, arrested Julie Dunaway as she juggled packages in an attempt to fit the key into the lock of her own door.

"Oh, hello, Ann," Julie smiled wearily, glancing briefly toward the jeans-clad figure leaping forward to prevent one bursting grocery bag from landing on the floor. Julie sighed with relief as she secured a hold on the remaining bag and began looking around for the key which had fallen during the exchange. Ann spied it and gave it a shove with her foot as Julie bent down and retrieved it.

"As usual I had to make a quick stop at the market so I'm a little later than usual. How about a cup of coffee? I'm dying for one." She fitted the key into the lock and pushed the door open, standing aside as Ann entered first. Once inside, she kicked the door closed with the heel of her foot.

"I know I've said this before, Julie, but you need to slow down, for heaven's sake! You work too hard." Directing her words over her shoulder, Ann headed familiarly for the nook which served as kitchen and bar. "You hardly ever take the time for anything special even on the weekends." Her concerned freckled face studied Julie, whose slim figure was bent low to set the bag on the floor. Ann placed her bag on the counter and searched Julie's face. "You'd better watch out, my friend, or you'll find yourself collapsed from overwork and underplay."

Julie chuckled, unable to feel offended at her friend's attitude. She knew Ann spoke from a genuine concern for her welfare.

"I know you mean well, Ann, but my work is enjoyable to me, and to be quite frank, I have an idea that things are not as good as they should be at the firm. If I can help Mr. Peters by doing a little work above what is strictly required, then I'm happy to do it." Julie's face stilled as her thoughts chased quickly to the early weeks of her employment at Peters-Winton Engineering. "After all, I owe him a lot for hiring me with so few qualifications."

Her friend's expression conveyed her opinion of Julie's modest statement. "You know very well that you've worked hard in your position at that firm, Julie. You don't really owe Mr. Peters anything except loyalty and a full day's work. You are going overboard when you stretch a day into ten hours or more."

Julie knew that Ann's remarks held more than a little good sense. But her amber eyes clouded as she allowed her thoughts to return to her work. There did seem to be something worrying Mr. Peters and although she certainly had no knowledge of the internal workings of the firm, she suspected he was more concerned than he let on.

She turned thoughtfully to her friend. "Of course, you're right to caution me about getting too involved with a job. But I'm sure Mr. Peters is worried about his firm. I don't have any idea what the trouble is, but I'm sure I'm right."

Ann clucked sympathetically as she began removing items from the bag. "Well, if he is in some sort of difficulty, I don't think he will look to his youngest staff employee for assistance. So if you want my advice," she continued, throwing a teasing look at Julie, "I still say you should take it a little easier and relax. Leave corporate problems to corporate people. After hours, that is."

Corporate people. Julie mused thoughtfully over the term. She certainly could not claim to be on that level of business management and she was not sure she wanted to be. She enjoyed her work and it successfully occupied her mind. She didn't really think of Frank Peters as the usual business tycoon either. He was a big, middle-aged man and had owned Peters-Winton Engineering since before Julie had been born. A friend of her father, he had been more than kind and generous to Julie two years before when she had badly needed a job. Throwing herself into the position offered by Mr. Peters, she had more than proved herself capable and successful. Actually, it was only a suspicion she had that all was not as it should be at the firm, but as most of her time and energy was spent there, she was unusually sensitive to the atmosphere at the office.

Briefly she allowed her thoughts to drift backward. If Mr. Peters were having trouble and it had to do with a more efficient management of his business, then there were professional people who dealt with that sort of thing. Thrusting aside these thoughts as they tended to lead to more painful personal ones, Julie gave a little shake of her head, unconsciously ridding her mind of any intrusions into an area that had long lain undisturbed. She wasn't going to get caught in that trap again, she vowed. Peters-Winton Engineering would have to get along without any suggestions from her in that line.

Hastily she marshalled her thoughts and with an effort concentrated on what Ann was saying.

"And I thought we could spend the weekend there. You could have a chance to relax and tramp around the woods. You know how you like that sort of thing. I promise you won't have to suffer the attentions of any men if you don't want to." She paused briefly, interrupting the rapid flow of words. "Julie! Have you heard anything I've said?"

Julie laughed guiltily. "Sorry, Ann, I did miss a few details." She placed a package in the cabinet and closed the door, turning to her friend whose hands propped on her hips betrayed an attitude of resigned exasperation. "I promise to listen this time," she placated. "What's it all about, now?"

Shaking her head helplessly, Ann repeated, "It's the Halsteads' lake cottage, and a very informal weekend guaranteed to make you forget your job and problems while overwhelming you with beautiful scenery and some very undemanding people." She checked them off on her slim, capable fingers. "Jim and me, the Halsteads and their two kids, and you. Nobody else. Now, promise me you will go."

"OK," Julie smiled, knowing she had disconcerted her friend with her immediate acceptance.

"I'm almost disappointed," Ann grumbled goodnaturedly. "I had a fool-proof argument rehearsed and now I'm all prepared and no one to persuade."

Julie stepped across the minute space from the

counter to the remainder of her cabinets to finish unpacking the last bag.

"Now for that coffee."

As Julie fussed with the coffee, Ann seated herself at the barstool opposite the stove top and considered the attractive picture which Julie made. With honey-streaked hair thick and curling softly at her shoulders and large amber eyes, she really was a beauty. Her cheekbones were sculpted high and would ensure her beauty even into old age. The wide vulnerable look which characterized her mouth was the perfect touch to lend her face femininity and feeling. Julie could have chosen any number of companions within their acquaintance and had no difficulty in enjoying a full and complete social life, but she expressed no interest outside of the passionate dedication to her job. It was almost, Ann thought musingly, as if she were devoid of the personal desires and longings which raged in most women. It was certain that past experience had wounded Julie deeply.

Julie was pouring the boiling water into the cups. She added sugar to Ann's and passed the cup over, unaware of the contemplative look her friend wore.

"I have begun to realize lately that I should get away from my work at least on weekends, Ann." Julie sipped her coffee thoughtfully. "I'm beginning to feel like a wind-up doll programmed to get up in the morning, go to work, come home in the evening, like a robot." She frowned thoughtfully into her coffee. "It's not that I'm bored with my work, but that there seems to be something missing. There must be something else." Fleetingly, a painful look crossed her face and her mouth trembled. More and more lately she suffered these momentary flashes of regret and bitterness. If only . . .

Jumping up, she opened the cookie jar and offered one to Ann whose sharp gaze was fastened on Julie's face. She needed to busy her hands when thoughts of what might have been began intruding. Lately such thoughts had impinged upon her consciousness in spite of her rigid determination to resist them. The weekend at the Halsteads' might be just what she needed to resolve the conflicting feelings which besieged her. She had made her decision two years ago and it was up to her to build a good life for herself. The weekend at the Halsteads' would be the beginning of broadening her narrow little world, she resolved. Successfully holding more painful thoughts aside, she eased back onto the stool and schooled her thoughts to listen to Ann's easy chatter.

It was late when Julie awakened the next morning. Friday. She gave a disgusted look at her clock radio, reminding herself that she had intended to have it repaired. Sometimes the alarm went awry and this morning that was obviously what happened.

Galvanizing into action, she hurriedly washed her face and brushed her teeth. Already her mind was occupied with several matters requiring her attention at the office. Applying makeup sparingly as always, she hastily put on a chocolate brown suit and cream blouse and dashed out of her apartment and down the hall.

Ordinarily the small car she found convenient for city driving proved dependable, and this morning was no exception. With a little luck, she would not be more than ten or fifteen minutes late. Turning out of the parking area reserved for tenants, she headed for downtown Boston.

Absently noting the city's skyline as she neared her destination, Julie was once again conscious of the charm of living in one of the most interesting and stimulating cities in America. Boston exuded a flavor all its own and more than once lately she had felt a bit guilty at not sampling some of the wonderful sights and experiences to be had in the historic old town. It had not been too long ago when she had delighted in discovering Boston, but that had been . . .

Feelings kept suppressed for a long time were clamoring to be released. Julie wondered how much longer she would be able to hold at bay bittersweet memories of the way it had been. She turned on the car radio to distract her thoughts. Almost as if in conspiracy with her own wayward imagination, the haunting strains of "The Way We Were" floated melodically, and for one devastating moment, tears blinded Julie's vision. What on earth was the matter with her? she asked herself angrily. Everything connected with that phase of her life had been successfully overcome. Why, all of a sudden, was she feeling anxious?

She leaned foward determinedly and turned the dial of the radio and at once the professional voice of a newscaster replaced the disturbing music. After a few moments, she was less agitated and nearing the location of the offices of Peters-Winton Engineering. Feeling relieved at the sight of the familiar stone building, she parked the car and rapidly ascended the steps.

When she entered her own working area, Candy

Wilson, a petite redhead, looked up and beamed a smile at Julie.

"Good morning," she said, rising from her cluttered desk and heading toward the coffee pot. "You look as though you need this."

Shrugging off her coat and hanging it on the rack, Julie returned the greeting and accepted the cup, sipping the hot liquid, savoring its taste.

"Thanks, Candy, you know I love my coffee and I really should try to drink less of it." She paused, taking another sip, then mischievously, "But not today."

They laughed together and Julie moved over to the door marked "Julia Dunaway—Administration." Entering her office, she placed the coffee on her desk and moved around to the chair. She sat down, picked up the papers left from the day before, and began to scan them.

Candy's voice interrupted her concentration. "Julie, you didn't give me a chance to tell you that Mr. Peters wants to see you as soon as you can arrange it this morning. He has a ten o'clock appointment and needs to discuss it with you before his visitor arrives."

Julie frowned, tiny lines marring her smooth forehead as she tried to recall whether or not she was supposed to be aware of Mr. Peters' appointment.

"OK, Candy, I'll be right there." She rose and moved around her desk. "The estimate on the Rhodes job should be finished today. Can you work the typing into your schedule?"

Her secretary nodded, reseating herself at her desk and flashing a quick smile at Julie. "I've already begun and it should be completed by noon, barring any disasters."

They had a good working relationship. Although sharing an informal camaraderie with Julie, Candy felt strong admiration and respect for her. Julie had, in less than two years, applied herself completely to her work and as a result, had risen rapidly from Mr. Peters' secretary to head of the Administrative Office. Many times Candy was aware that Julie devoted more time and effort to the job than many employees would care to. It had sometimes seemed that Julie had no other life except her work.

Exiting her own office, Julie entered the hall and headed toward the suite of offices where Mr. Peters was located. She paused in the reception area, and after greeting the secretary, she knocked briefly on the door marked "private." Hearing a muffled reply, she turned the handle and entered.

"Good morning, Julie." Frank Peters' friendly countenance beamed at his favorite employee. "I'm glad to see you looking as beautiful as usual." Waving a hand toward a chair upholstered in brown leather, he indicated that Julie should sit down.

"I don't know whether you have been aware of it, Julie," Mr. Peters began, "but with rising costs and labor problems, my firm has been experiencing some poor profits lately. I've tried to cope with these circumstances myself, but I'm getting older and perhaps some of my techniques are a bit dated or less effective than they could be." He twiddled with the pen on his desk and rearranged several articles as he searched for further words.

Julie felt a momentary twinge of alarm and braced herself anxiously.

Mr. Peters was continuing. "I was floundering around trying to work out these problems myself when a letter arrived offering a professional approach to my dilemma. I've had a few preliminary discussions with this firm and I'm convinced they have the answer to what ails Peters-Winton," he finished with a flourish.

"You certainly sound optimistic, Mr. Peters," Julie offered, still a little vague as to exactly what he was talking about. "Of course you know you can count on me to help in any way I can."

"Now, my dear, I'm glad to hear that, because I've a special little favor to ask of you because of your unique position in the firm." Mr. Peters leaned back and looked at Julie expectantly.

Julie waited.

"When these people come into a firm," he explained, "they need complete information as to its functions, personnel, contracts pending . . . you know the sort of thing. They also need a person within the organization who knows its operation backward and forward. Of course, as my former secretary, and now as my administration manager, you would be that person. Julie, I hope you will agree to work with Mr. Brandt in whatever capacity is necessary."

For a moment Julie's mind failed to register the implications in Mr. Peters' request. The only thing which had registered was the name Brandt and it stunned her brain momentarily. Her stomach curled unpleasantly. Then, pulling herself together mentally, she forced her attention to what Mr. Peters was saying.

"I'm expecting him any minute now and since you will be working closely with him every day, I wanted to introduce you first. As a matter of fact, he asked to be assisted by the administration manager and, of course, that would be you. My other department heads have been advised that I am considering this action, but they can meet him and his staff later." Oblivious to Julie's shaken composure, Mr. Peters rambled on confidently. "Actually I plan a little gathering this evening just for that purpose."

The buzzer on the intercom sounded and he spoke into it, issuing instructions to his secretary. Rising, he prepared to greet the visitor. With a growing sense of dread, Julie turned as the door opened.

The man who entered was every bit as masterful and compelling as Julie remembered. In a gray business suit with an immaculate white shirt and tie of muted stripes, he looked every inch the successful male. His dark hair and strong features were devastatingly attractive and against his deeply tanned face, his gray eyes were startling. Mr. Peters smilingly welcomed him into the office with a hearty handshake and greeting.

Julie had no chance to bring her reeling senses under control. She raised her eyes to his, feeling a jolt as she encountered the cold stare of her husband.

"Julie," Mr. Peters' voice barely penetrated her chaotic thoughts. "It's a real pleasure to introduce you to Alex Brandt, a management consultant outstanding in his field. Alex is going to put us right back on the road to success!" Turning to Alex, "This is Julie Dunaway, my girl Friday and administration manager, who you will find invaluable as you look over our operation." Mr. Peters turned proudly to his stunned employee, waiting for her acknowledgement of Alex Brandt.

Stricken dumb, Julie could only stare. Alex himself merely nodded politely. With a tight smile, he murmured a vague greeting, not indicating by the slightest flicker that he recognized Julie, let alone that she was his wife of two and a half years.

"Julie Dunaway," he repeated distantly and only Julie was aware of the slight emphasis on her last name.

Trembling, Julie stood and offered her hand. "How do you do, Mr. Brandt," she faltered, not sure whether their association was to be revealed or whether Alex had completely eliminated her from his life and treated the past as if it had never been.

She winced as his warm hand enclosed hers briefly but painfully hard.

Mr. Peters, failing to sense any unusual vibrations, prepared to go. "Why don't I just leave you two together as you discuss what Alex needs and how to go about it." He turned to Julie. "Alex has been informed that you will be at his complete disposal while he is here, Julie." Then he ushered them inside and gestured toward the long conference table and chairs. "Feel free to make complete use of my conference room," he offered, "and if you require anything," to Alex, "just ask. Julie is a whiz at making things happen around here. That's why I am pleased to have her assist you, Alex." Beaming optimistically, he backed out of the room, closing the door behind him.

"What are you doing here?" Julie whispered angrily in the cold silence which followed Mr. Peters' departure.

Alex returned her look with a complacent one of his own. "I should have thought the firm's 'whiz' would have comprehended my reason for being here. Obviously, I have been retained to try to figure out why this firm is no longer making a profit."

"You know what I mean," Julie snapped impatiently, resisting the urge to slap the infuriating assurance off his face. It had always been that way with them; their arguments, and there had been plenty of them, had been as violent as their passion. No one had ever been able to reduce Julie to incoherent rage as effectively as Alex. And Alex had been very susceptible to anger himself when touched off by what he had called Julie's unreasonable tantrums.

"Why are you here, Alex? I know your firm is excellently staffed. You could have deputized any number of your people to handle this." Julie was making a strong effort to keep her voice even, to conquer the anger and fear which threatened to surface. Under no circumstance would she let him know just how shattered she was to see him. For the past two years she had felt nothing regarding her brief and ill-fated marriage. Even when the thought of Alex had intruded, any emotion had been firmly stifled. It was almost as though her heart was in cold storage while her mind and body worked furiously in an effort to make a life for herself alone. But now, at the first appearance of the very person whose memory she worked desperately to erase, all the feeling and fear carefully blocked came flooding back as intensely as ever.

Drawing a deep breath, she faced him squarely. "I suppose if we must work together, then we might as well get on with it. How do you want to begin?"

Alex directed a long, straight look at her, his eyes hooded as he regarded her flushed, angry face. She had a feeling that he knew exactly what havoc he was causing. For a moment, she felt that he was almost pleased, even satisfied that she had reacted so strongly to his sudden appearance. Giving herself a mental shake, Julie pulled herself together.

"Well, I'm waiting. It seems you're the boss!"

Alex had been resting his long length against the table during their heated exchange, his thighs firm and strong even in a relaxed stance. Involuntarily, a vision of his body without the trappings of a business suit flashed swiftly across Julie's consciousness. He had a beautiful body. His wide shoulders, perfectly muscled, tapered to a slim waist and hips.

Horrified, she realized just where her thoughts were leading. It was impossible to stay in the room with him. She rushed toward the door, fleeing the betraying memories as much as his physical presence. She grabbed for the handle.

Alex was beside her in an instant and his hand closed around her wrist in a punishing grip. His face was close, too close, and his breath brushed her face as he forcibly restrained her.

"Come back here, you little fool! If you run out of here in a panic, how are you going to explain your behavior to Peters?" he grated. "Won't it seem odd that a total stranger," with a bitter emphasis on the last two words, "frightened you so badly in only ten minutes that you took to your heels?"

"Take your hands off me!" Julie cried, struggling to free her arm. "I hate you! I can't stand the sight of you!"

Alex released her wrist and grabbed both her shoulders in his hands, holding her steadily. "For God's sake, Julie! What do you think I intend to do, ravage you right here, within twelve feet of your employer?" Dropping his hands so quickly that she nearly lost her balance, he pulled one of the chairs away from the table and flung himself into it, pushing his legs straight out in front of him. Reaching into his inside jacket pocket, he pulled out cigarettes and placing one in his mouth, he dug in his pocket for a light. He snapped it quickly, lighting the cigarette and inhaling deeply.

Julie watched him warily, unsure of what would happen next. The explosive atmosphere in the room caused her stomach to tighten and she walked shakily over to the coffee pot and poured a cup for herself. Cradling the cup in both hands and finding some comfort in its warmth, she sipped the drink, grateful for something to do while she brought her scattered senses under control and tried to think what to do in her impossible situation.

"Well," Alex laughed humorlessly, "ten minutes together and we're at each other's throats. Just like old times."

"I didn't ask you to come here," Julie replied defensively, "and I can hardly be expected to welcome you with open arms considering the circumstances."

"I wouldn't expect you to open your arms to me under any circumstances," Alex bit out savagely. "Luckily, you won't ever get the chance again, either." Then sitting up suddenly in his chair he leaned over and pulled out one for Julie, indicating wearily that she should sit down. "This isn't getting us anywhere and I didn't come here this morning to fight with you. I've had all of that I can take for a lifetime."

Julie winced inwardly. Alex still had the power to wound her, but she mustn't ever let him suspect it.

"What is the great Alex Brandt doing here?" she asked, taking refuge in sarcasm.

Alex drew a deep breath. "It's as simple as this, Julie." He looked directly at her and she was unable to read the blank look in the cool, gray eyes. "I'm here to do a job. Peters has assigned you as the most knowledgeable person to fill me in on the particulars of his firm." He raked his hands through his dark hair, causing it to spring crisply back into shape. "Although we have our personal differences, I have nothing but respect for your professional abilities and I do need your cooperation." He paused a moment, his eyes never leaving her face. "Now, can we get on with it?"

Julie rose from her chair. Heading to the coffee pot, she asked over her shoulder, "Would you like some coffee?" Reaching for a clean cup without waiting for an answer, she began to pour.

"Well," Alex urged impatiently when she did not respond.

"I don't have any choice, as you well know," she replied quietly, placing the cup on the table in front of him. "Where do we start?"

Subjecting her to more silent regard, Alex instantly switched from personal issues to the business at hand. He became every inch the successful management consultant.

"I will need to see a list of all employees and a brief description of their job responsibilities," he began. "Also, progress reports on contracts in work and those pending." In a no-nonsense manner, he began to inform her of what was needed. "Shouldn't you be making a list, or do you intend to retain this in your head?"

Flashing him a suspicious look, Julie saw that his question was not meant sarcastically but was part of the complete attention he brought to his work and his insistence that his instructions be carried out. The violent scene just minutes ago was completely pushed out of his mind as if it had never occurred. She stared at him wordlessly for a moment.

"Right," she replied. "I'll just run down and get a few things which should help you get started." She turned to him tentatively. "And I will pick up paper and pencil for taking notes." Reaching the door, she opened it and headed for her own office.

Julie was impressed during the course of the day with the scope and amount of progress made by Alex. Working steadily through until lunchtime, he proceeded to familiarize himself with Peters-Winton and he shot questions at her with rapid-fire speed and expected concise, knowledgeable answers. More than once she was absurdly pleased that she had succeeded in satisfying his demands. A couple of times she had even sensed he was a tiny bit impressed with her answers.

By unspoken agreement, no mention of anything remotely personal was made by either of them. Julie found herself wondering about his life during the past two years, but by and large he kept her so busy that very litttle time was left to draw any conclusions. His work had always played a vital role in his life. Bitterly Julie recalled that in the end, it had been the most important thing in his life. Certainly *she* had not rated a very high place.

After lunch, which Julie had managed to avoid having with Alex, she was once again summoned into Mr. Peters' office. Entering, she saw that Alex was already there and braced herself for another session with him.

"Well, Julie, Alex tells me you two are working well as a team and I can tell you I'm not at all surprised." Mr. Peters' satisfaction showed in every word. *The irony of it all*, Julie thought, *that Alex and I make a good team.*

"Alex will be bringing in a couple of his staff people," Mr. Peters continued, "and tonight I plan to have everyone over to my house for drinks just to get acquainted. Then Monday morning, we'll be ready to start full steam."

With a feeling of dismay, Julie surveyed the two men. "But, Mr. Peters, I had planned a weekend trip with some friends and we were to leave this evening right after work." Feeling an unreasonable sense of guilt, but desperate to avoid any contact with Alex that was not absolutely necessary, Julie faced the two men. Alex was looking bored and Mr. Peters was openly disappointed.

"Julie, you know I would never request you to cancel any personal plans except for a really good reason," he began, "but this little thing tonight won't take very long and you could run down to your weekend place bright and early tomorrow morning. Alex has suggested this and feels that a preliminary meeting with all the staff involved will start us off right," he finished. "And, he's the expert!"

Julie shot an indignant look at the "expert" whose expression was totally unreadable. He met her eyes with a bland look.

"Of course," he drawled, "if Miss Dunaway has important plans, then we wouldn't want to be responsible for ruining them. Looks like we'll have to meet tonight without your project coordinator, Frank."

If that wasn't just like Alex, Julie fumed inwardly. Somehow or other he had insinuated her weekend plans were frivolous, and he made it seem an unnecessary selfish act on her part in ignoring her employer's request to get this project off on the right foot.

Not willing to capitulate too quickly, Julie replied reasonably, "Naturally my plans for leaving this evening aren't absolutely vital." She glared at Alex. "And of course, I want to do my part to ensure the success of your work, Mr. Brandt, but I did make my plans some days ago," she lied. "However, if you feel I am absolutely necessary to the success of your plan, I suppose I can arrange to leave tomorrow morning instead," she finished sweetly.

Acknowledging this round to her, Alex inclined his head slightly, his eyes glinting a promise of later retribution.

"Well, that's generous of you, my dear," Mr. Peters said heartily. "If all my employees were as dedicated as you, I might not be in this mess today." Turning to Alex, "Since you say you will not be needing Julie again today, I see no reason to detain her any longer."

With a smile he watched as Julie prepared to leave them.

She was suddenly stopped by Alex's deep voice.

"Oh, Miss Dunaway," he said in a silky tone.

Julie halted, her body tensed for his next words.

"Why don't I drop by your place this evening on my way to Frank's house and give you a lift?"

Her mouth opened to protest but was forestalled by Mr. Peters' pleased exclamation. "That's very thoughtful of you to suggest giving Julie a lift, Alex," he declared enthusiastically, not noticing the angry indignation directed toward Alex by a far from grateful Julie. "I feel a bit responsible for this young lady," he continued, smiling down at her fondly, "and she does have to drive across town to reach my place. Since we sort of railroaded her into coming tonight, the least we can do is provide her transportation."

"It is absolutely unnecessary," Julie stated flatly. Nothing would induce her to get in a car with him. Talk about being railroaded! A quick glance at Alex revealed that he was waiting with amused interest to see how she would contrive to avoid his suggestion.

"I frequently drive after dark all over the metropolitan area," she argued. "I have never had a moment's trouble."

"But, my dear, this was my idea," Mr. Peters inserted reasonably, "and it would be thoughtless and inconsiderate not to arrange your transportation."

Julie's shoulders momentarily sagged in defeat as she realized that further objections would sound churlish and possibly arouse curiosity if she continued to object.

"That's settled then," came Alex's voice, brisk and businesslike. Although she shot him a sharp glance, there seemed no trace of smugness about him as their eyes met. Once again meeting a blank look, she had a fleeting impression of having been manipulated. Turning on her heel, she left them without another word, closing the door quietly and firmly behind her.

Thankful to be back at her own desk, Julie considered the situation. The last thing she had expected when she drove to work was that she would be working alongside her own husband. It was unbelievable, almost as if the restless thoughts and memories she had been having lately had somehow conjured him up. She should have done the logical thing and filed for a divorce. If she had, she would be a free woman and not bound to a man she despised who still had the power to antagonize and wound her in spite of all that had happened.

Julie stood up and walked to the window. Peering out, she was unaware of the busy scene below her but was remembering the past.

Chapter Two

How well she remembered her first glimpse of Alex
Brandt. She had been employed as a secretary, but
finding the work less challenging than she would
have liked, she had enrolled in college night courses.
In one of them, a business course, the instructor
arranged to have professional businessmen speak
occasionally so that students could benefit from
actual experience. This particular night Alex Brandt
was introduced to the class. There were only twelve
students; perhaps that was why he had noticed her.
She found him overwhelmingly attractive in a camel
corduroy sportcoat and white turtleneck sweater
with black slacks. Her immediate reaction to Alex's
sheer maleness had puzzled and disconcerted her.
Not given to that sort of thing she wrestled with her
feelings throughout the evening. Alex's face was
rough-hewn with strongly defined cheekbones and a
tough, square chin. But it was his eyes that caught
and held her like a magnet. They were gray and
piercing, the whites startling against the brown of his
skin. Black hair, hopelessly curly, grew thick and
crisp over his well-shaped head. Later she came to
know that it was a source of bother to him that curls
would spring out rebelliously no matter how vigor-

ously he brushed them down and no matter how good a haircut he had.

That night she had noticed all these things and they had combined to enchant her. He was an obvious success as a guest speaker and had been a favorite of the class. During the entire time he spoke, he had repeatedly singled Julie out. He smiled at her and several times he seemed to direct his attention to her.

At the end of the class period, she stayed with several of the other students to speak to him. She told herself it was because he was an interesting speaker and that she had been impressed with the content of his words. But deep down, even then, she had known she found the man himself irresistible.

She waited until all the other students had spoken to him and he turned those wonderful eyes on her, smiling slightly. "Thank you, Mr. Brandt, for a very informative hour." Flushed and nervous, she was hardly aware of anything more than his compelling gaze. "You make the business world seem intriguing."

"To me it is intriguing, Miss . . . ?" He paused expectantly.

"Dunaway, Julie Dunaway."

"Miss Julie Dunaway," he repeated. Then, unbelievably, "Would you have dinner with me tomorrow night?"

She gasped at the suddenness of it, then laughed delightedly. "I'd love it!"

Smiling, he ushered her toward the door of the classroom. "Fine. I'll pick you up," he paused, "at what address?"

She told him.

"Good. See you then, about seven thirty."

She nodded, slightly dazed.

Gently propelling her through the doorway, he turned in the opposite direction and with a wave of his hand, disappeared down the corridor.

She dressed with particular care for her first date. She chose a mauve silk blouse with a plunging neckline where she hung lightweight gold chains of varying lengths. A deep plum velvet skirt completed the outfit, with shoes of a matching color whose high heels gave her a feeling of elegance as she walked. Her hair was brushed into a loose tumble of amber curls around her face but pulled away and pinned with a jeweled comb on one side, baring one perfect ear. Tiny gold rings in her ears added just the right touch.

Her tawny eyes were shining with excitement when the doorbell rang and she opened the door to admit Alex for the first time. In a navy blue blazer with gold buttons and gray slacks, he was compellingly handsome to her dazzled eyes. The shirt he wore was of the same pale gray as his eyes and the stripes on his tie were dark blue and gray.

They looked at each other for a long moment; Alex's eyes darkening at Julie's golden beauty.

"You look wonderful," he smiled slowly. His mouth, she noticed, was sensual, the bottom lip full and generous.

"Thank you. You look pretty sharp yourself," she said lightly, trying for some poise but feeling like a schoolgirl on a first date.

"Would you like a drink before we go?" Wetting her lips, she moved slightly so that he could come inside.

He stepped in and looked around with one comprehensive glance. She felt even then that his personality was such that he sized up any situation or person just as comprehensively and quickly, and she shivered.

"Show me where they are and I'll mix the drinks," he offered, taking charge effortlessly.

They drank their drinks and Julie's feeling of being inexorably drawn toward something as yet unknown but inevitable increased. Alex seated himself comfortably on the sofa and Julie perched on a little chair across from him. He inquired about her family but was not forthcoming about his own background. Julie, in her growing happiness, knew they had all the time in the world to learn about each other.

Drinks finished, they left the apartment and entered the street, not particularly noticing the nip in the still chilly weather or Boston's early spring.

His car was low slung and powerful, as Julie had known it would be. He drove directly to a cozy, little restaurant south of the city where the food was heavenly. During dinner they talked, laughed and drank a bottle of wine. When Alex had been assured that she couldn't eat another thing, they left the dining room and wandered up some iron stairs to an intimate little bar decorated in an old nautical theme and resembling the crow's nest of an old ship. A few couples were dancing on the tiny area to one side of the room and Alex drew her onto the floor and into his arms.

"I've been waiting all night for this," he murmured with his lips close to her ear. Time stood still for Julie. If it was possible to fall in love at first sight, then she had done so, as crazy as it might be.

* * *

That first night neither spoke as Julie searched through her purse for the key to her apartment. Finally, Alex purposefully lifted it from her hands. Then still holding onto her purse, took both her hands in his and moved them slowly around behind her back. She was drawn completely up against his chest. With her face pressed into his shirt, she heard the warm, steady beat of his heart and felt the warmth of his body, his masculine smell invading her senses. Never before had Julie felt such a strong desire to be kissed. Quite unconsciously she raised her face to his and he lowered his mouth.

Delight, unknown to her until then, was hers. Tenderly at first, he tasted her lips, moving from one corner to the other, teasing her lips open. Then he urgently took possession, probing the warmth within, deepening the kiss into an invasion of her very being. Absolutely mindless by now, Julie let him have his way, submitting with a languorous feeling induced by his total expertise. His hands gently stroked her back, warm and caressing through the thin material of her blouse, bringing her ever closer, molding her to his body, crushing her breasts against his chest. Breaking the kiss, he buried his face in the softness of her neck, feathering light kisses down the curve where her shoulder began. At the slight pressure of his hands, Julie dropped her head back, baring her throat to his invading lips. Gathering her even closer, he ran his mouth down to the cleft of her breasts where her silken blouse parted.

With a little gasp of pleasure, her arms lifted to cradle his head, reveling in the feel of his crisp hair and the warmth of his strong neck.

"Julie, Julie," he whispered, his lips returning to

her face, kissing her eyes, her temples, moving to
her ears where with his tongue he evoked sensuous
delight. She clasped her arms tightly around his
neck. They were so close that she could feel the
tremor of his body as desire swamped them both.

He withdrew slightly, drawing an unsteady breath.
Still holding her closely, he gently rested his forehead against hers. "Much as I would like to, I don't
think it would be a good idea for me to come
inside," he whispered huskily.

Bemused and still aroused, Julie failed to compre-
hend for a moment. Then, recalling where she was,
she looked down shyly, flushed and uncertain as
Alex reluctantly removed his arms and leaned over
to unlock and open the door.

He placed her purse into her hands, gave her a
light kiss on her nose, and gently nudged her inside.
His softly whispered, "good night," followed by the
click of the door, signified the end of a perfect
evening.

That had been the beginning of their brief and
rapturous courtship. Alex filled her with joy, his
interests fascinated her, and his opinion on everything never failed to intrigue her. He was knowledgeable on a wide range of subjects and since he
was already thirty years old, he was experienced in
the ways of the world.

He was an only son. His father had been an
eminently respected judge and Alex had studied law,
mostly, he said, to please his parents. But his father
died when Alex had been practicing only a few
months, and as business and commerce were his real
passions, he entered a prestigious firm of efficiency
experts and proved his business acumen with

rapid speed. It was characteristic of him that all his energy and determination were focused on learning his chosen profession and rising to a full partnership within a few years. It had been Alex's idea to enlarge the scope of the firm to include management consulting in its services. By placing a team of experts in an ailing business, excesses and inefficiencies of both personnel and methods were pinpointed. Reorganization and success inevitably followed. Such singularity of purpose was typical of him, and since he was willing to work as hard as he required his staff to work, he had attained an astonishing amount of success in a relatively short number of years.

His mother, however, nursed an undying sense of disappointment that he had not chosen to follow his father's prestigious footsteps. Since he had distinguished himself in his studies at the university and had practiced law for a short length of time, she still dreamed that he would return to "his real profession" in time. An autocratic woman, Boston born and bred, she cherished the hope that Alex would, if left alone, get his fill of the business world and return to the bar and ultimately a judgeship like his father. She had even selected the correct wife for him.

Julie was blissfully unaware of most of Alex's background during the early weeks of their acquaintance, but with their growing love, Alex wanted to take her home to meet his mother.

On the rainy afternoon that Julie met Alex's mother, they entered the room breathless and laughing, their clothes damp and clinging from the dash from garage to house. Mrs. Brandt met them at the door.

Alex made the introduction. "Mother, this is Julie, the girl I love and plan to marry."

Turning to Mrs. Brandt, Julie was jolted by the dislike in the older woman's eyes. She had a tight smile on her lips, however, and apparently Alex noticed nothing. Julie held out her hand and felt the cold clasp of her future mother-in-law. Bewildered by the unexpected hostility, she moved back uncertainly to the security of Alex's side. As long as he loved her, she needn't fear this woman, she thought. It was as well that she could not know the futility of her thoughts then.

The late afternoon sun slanted its rays through the window of her office and the sounds of closing time recalled Julie to her surroundings. Good-byes, flung cheerfully on this Friday afternoon, echoed up and down the hall.

Candy poked her head around the door and seeing Julie unusually still at the window moved hesitantly into the office, her face mirroring the concern in her voice.

"Julie, are you feeling alright?"

Arranging her features in a slightly stiff smile, Julie faced her secretary. "Yes, Candy, I'm alright. Just glad it's Friday." Nervously, she stepped up to her desk and began an unnecessary shuffling of the papers spread on its surface. Keeping her face down, she continued, "What do you say we wrap it up for the week?"

Still sensing that something was awry, Candy stood uncertainly.

"Nothing is wrong, Candy. I've had a long week and now I'm really looking forward to a lazy weekend." She laughed reassuringly. "I guess I was just anticipating doing nothing when you came in and caught me."

Not quite satisfied, but knowing that Julie would reveal nothing more, Candy turned to leave. "I'll see you Monday, then. Hope you have a good weekend. You certainly deserve it!" A few moments later, the sound of the door closing signified her departure.

Quickly Julie gathered her own belongings and grabbing her coat, closed and locked her office. Suddenly it was imperative that she leave. She had been unaware of the passing of time as she stood lost in memories of the past, but if she was not fast, she might be forced into another confrontation with the flesh and blood Alex. And she did not feel able to cope with his overpowering tactics. Soon enough her defenses would be tested again and from the way things had gone during their meeting anything could happen. Such haste proved unnecessary, however, as she did not encounter Alex on her way to her car.

An hour later she unlocked the door to her apartment and let herself in. Once inside she subsided into a comfortable chair, kicking off her shoes and leaning her head back wearily. More than anything she wished she did not have to meet Alex again. Earlier she had called Ann Lawson to explain what had happened and to let her know she would be arriving at the cottage on Saturday morning. She had omitted any mention of Alex. Ann knew about her marriage and until they split up she had known and been very fond of Alex. Julie never revealed the reasons for the sudden end to her marriage, but Ann had proved to be a real support to her at a time when she had badly needed it. Ann had even been responsible for finding Julie's apartment. Had she known that Alex was back in Julie's life, she would have been worried and concerned, might even have offered to delay her own plans for the weekend. But

Julie was determined that she not know and would have no opportunity to cause Ann and her fiancé to miss any part of their enjoyable weekend.

Reluctantly getting up from the chair, Julie moved into her bedroom where, with a glance at the bedside clock, she began removing her clothes. A hot bath with lots of bath salts would refresh her, she thought longingly. Entering the small tiled bathroom, she turned on the taps.

Later she emerged warm and fragrant and more relaxed than she had been all day. Clad only in a short terry robe, she sank down onto the bed and lay back to rest for a few minutes before getting dressed. The next thing she knew, the doorbell was ringing insistently. Realizing that she had been hearing it from the edge of sleep in her mind for some time, she stumbled to the door.

"Julie, are you in there?"

Alex! What time was it? Dazed, she fumbled at the chain, unlocked the door and opened it to an impatient Alex, his broad shoulders and imposing height threatening as she became aware of how scantily her body was clothed.

"Looks like you aren't quite ready," he drawled, running his eyes over her hair, hastily pulled on top of her head, tendrils escaping to trail along her delicate temples and nape. Slowly he assessed the entire length of her, lingering at the cleft of her breasts and down long, golden legs, smooth and perfectly formed.

"Julie," he murmured, his eyes resting on her face and focusing on her soft mouth, "you're even more beautiful than I remembered." He kicked the door closed behind him and reached for her.

Still confused from her abrupt awakening, Julie

didn't immediately resist as she realized Alex's intent. His arms came around her like steel bands and his mouth came down on hers bent on possession.

Forcing her lips open, he kissed her deeply with a desperate hunger. She was drowning in the pure sensual delight of sensations long denied. With one hand, he shoved aside her robe at the collar and plunged inside, his fingers closing warmly around the firm, tip-tilted peaks. His touch induced a fiery pleasure and heat rushed to her brain as with sensual expertise he fondled each breast, his mouth never leaving hers. Suddenly he reached to lift her and Julie came to her senses. Struggling and sobbing with a mixture of rage and unsatisfied desire, she jerked away from his hands, only succeeding as Alex was momentarily weakened with the force of his desire, slightly reeling, his face flushed. She faced him, desperately pulling her robe into place and securing the tiebelt with trembling fingers.

"I might have known this is what you had in mind when you so considerately offered to drive me tonight." Quietly controlled, bitterly accusing, she surveyed him.

Clamping his jaw tensely, Alex turned away struggling to regain control. He was breathing hard as though he had been running. He swore softly. "I know you won't believe this," he began heavily, "but I swear to you I did not intend to do that." He faced her squarely, his gray eyes darkened almost to black. "But when you came to the door, all flushed and barely awake," he laughed bitterly, "I couldn't help myself."

Tears welled as the pain of loss and regret washed over Julie. Strangely enough she was no longer angry. She turned abruptly without another word and walked into her bedroom, closing the door firmly behind her.

She dressed quickly and went out to meet Alex. His look as she came toward him was veiled and enigmatic. He was in complete control again, his face impassive. It was impossible to tell what he was thinking, impossible to believe that a bare ten minutes ago he had been passionately aroused, demanding and receiving a response from her that no other man was capable of evoking.

Neither spoke as Julie selected a wrap from a closet and, holding it in her hands, avoided his touch as they turned out the lights and left.

Most of the guests at Frank Peters' home were familiar to Julie as they were staff members. After greeting their host, Alex placed a firm hand under her elbow and guided her over to two men standing at a table laden with a luscious selection of hors d'oeuvres.

"Julie, meet James Richards and Wes Blakeney, my two cohorts in crime," he greeted them warmly, extending his hand and grasping each of theirs in turn. "If you guys can tear yourselves away from food for a moment, I want you to meet Julie Dunaway, Frank Peters' administrative manager and an old friend of mine. Better be on your best behavior because she can make or break our success on this one." The look he turned on Julie caused her heart to accelerate.

The two men grinned good-naturedly and looked at Julie, admiration plain in their eyes. The one called Wes whistled softly but appreciatively. "I'll bet it won't matter whether we're nice tonight or not, Miss Dunaway," his grin swung to Alex, "the boss will be saving you for himself, you can bet."

Alex remained silent, but the glint in his eyes must have been clearly evident to both men. He moved off taking Julie with him.

"Don't let those guys fool you. They are both as sharp as they need to be when it comes to getting a job done." He was obviously sincere in his praise of his men and Julie was once again reminded of the qualities which had made her fall in love with Alex in the first place.

Frank Peters was motioning for them to join him at the other side of the room, and as they reached his side, Julie noticed several of his staff members eyeing Alex curiously.

"You'll probably be talking with John Fisher here," he began, indicating a tall, stoop-shouldered man with thinning hair and glasses who stood silently at his side. "He is vital to me in his capacity as contracts manager." Fisher extended his hand to Alex, then nodded coolly to Julie. She had never felt entirely comfortable with Fisher. He was reticent during office hours and nothing was known of his private life. Mr. Peters was explaining that Fisher was instrumental in compiling bid packages in competition with other engineering firms with the contracts then awarded to the lowest bidder. It was certainly accurate that his function was a vital one to Peters-Winton.

One by one, each member of Mr. Peters' staff was presented to Alex who acknowledged each one politely. Julie, who knew him well, noted that he assessed each man sharply and no doubt accurately.

Alex was never very far from her side that evening, a fact which puzzled Julie, although he addressed her directly very little and then only with a conventional "pass the salt," or "will you have ham or shrimp rolls." All in all, it was an uncomfortable evening. The scene at her apartment which preceded it lingered in her subconsciousness.

Once in the car, however, he seemed remote and preoccupied. Unwillingly, she conceded that it was possible he hadn't intended seduction when he had arranged to escort her for the evening. Perhaps old habits die hard, she thought painfully, and the sight of her in dishabille had awakened memories of the passion which had always flared easily between them.

The aching in her head increased as her thoughts churned, and she reached up to rub the tips of her fingers against her throbbing temples.

"Headache?" Alex's voice reached her through the pain.

"A little."

"I'll have you home in a few minutes. Do you have something to take?"

Startled by the unexpected concern, Julie threw him a quick look, her eyes wide. Aware that she was staring, he turned his head, their eyes meeting briefly before he turned his attention back to driving.

"Well, do you have something you can take?"

"I have some aspirin. That's all I need." Julie wondered hysterically if perhaps there wasn't some obscure lesson to be learned. There they were, husband and wife after a separation of two years, he solicitously inquiring about her headache and she responding just like they were a normal couple. It really boggled the mind. She felt as though she had suddenly been picked up and put into another world since meeting Alex again. She felt as though control of her own destiny was being taken out of her own hands.

Pulling neatly into the side curb, Alex stopped the car and turned to Julie. "There was something I wanted to talk to you about, Julie." His voice was deep and he seemed uncharacteristically tentative and uncertain. "Since you have something planned for the weekend, perhaps it's better to wait until you get back." His eyes stared unseeing past Julie's shoulders into the blackness beyond. He opened his lips to continue, then as if changing his mind he suddenly clamped them tightly shut. Shifting his weight he opened the car door, slamming it behind him, and walked around to Julie's side.

Confused and head pounding, she allowed him to help her out of the car and they walked up the steps of the brownstone in silence. After she had located the key from her handbag, Alex took it from her unresisting hand and fitted it into the door, pushing it open to allow her to precede him. He followed her inside.

Turning back, she began a protest, but he stopped her with a clipped, "Don't worry. I have no intention of resuming what I began earlier this evening."

Julie's shoulders drooped, fatigue and pain evident in her drawn face. Alex's face softened suddenly and, dragging his fingers through his hair, he urged, "Go get undressed, Julie, while I locate the aspirin and a glass of water." Making himself at home, he took off his coat and slung it over the back of a chair. Seeing that she still stood uncertainly in the middle of the room, he moved over to her, drew off the thin gossamer shawl she had used as a wrap, and gently pushed her toward her bedroom door.

Tears welled in her eyes, temporarily blinding her as she submitted. It was inexpressibly comforting to allow someone else to take charge, relieving her of the necessity of having to do anything, if only for a little while. Tonight she did not feel able to cope with the sudden complications that had beset her since that morning. Fleetingly, as she stepped out of her dress and hastily removed her makeup, she wondered whether she could resist Alex if he should decide not to leave her in peace. Pulling down the covers and crawling between the sheets, she did not even have the strength to think about it.

Alex came into the room and silently proffered two white tablets which she swallowed obligingly with a few mouthfuls of water. Then sinking back onto the pillow, she closed her eyes, hardly conscious of his presence. Unaware of the vulnerability of her face, taut with pain, lashes long and curling against her cheeks, she drew her knees up, turning her head into the pillow and trying to escape the pain.

Alex's hands came down on her shoulders and she threw a startled, wary look into his face.

"Just turn over, Julie. I only want to help."

Unable to object, Julie turned onto her stomach and when Alex's hands touched her shoulders, in spite of the pain, a shiver curled down her spine. He slipped the strings of her gown off her shoulders and his hands began a magic of their own, hard fingers kneading in just the right place, cupping under her nape, fanning out along her spine, smoothing away the tension of knotted muscles. Silently and rhythmically he worked. The only sound was the sound of his breathing, steady and deep, feathering her skin warmly now and then. She moaned softly with blessed relief and was drifting into sleep when Alex pulled the bedclothes up around her shoulders and departed.

The weekend at the cottage in Maine passed peacefully in a series of long walks in woods coming alive with flowering trees and the springtime sounds of birds and animals. Ann and her fiancé Jim Erickson were quite content with their own company and preoccupied with plans for their upcoming wedding. Gratefully, Julie was left to her own devices.

There was plenty for her to think about. The sudden appearance of Alex into her life had affected her more than she ever dreamed it would. Naturally, she had known that some day a reckoning between them would come but her reaction to him had surprised and frightened her with its intensity. Trudging through the woods, she pondered her unbridled response to Alex. He still had the power to anger her and unwittingly came the thought that he could still arouse her.

How was it that knowing as she did that he was untrustworthy and selfish and self-centered to the point of arrogance, when he looked at her in his lazy, languorous way, her breathing quickened and she was assailed by memories of the rapture they had shared. How perfect their physical union had been and how unspeakable the pain when it had all fallen apart.

What could he have to talk to her about? Although the events of the night before were somewhat vague, she recalled something about waiting until this weekend was over to discuss . . . what? Could it have something to do with their marriage? Suddenly, a new thought struck. Was he going to ask her to start divorce proceedings? Had he found someone else? Strangely enough, she had never allowed herself to think of the possibility that Alex would fall in love and want to marry again. In the two years they had been apart she had so successfully prevented thoughts of him from intruding that now she realized with sudden clarity that she would hate Alex to marry someone else. She simply had not permitted herself to think about him because thoughts of their lost love were so painful.

Unwillingly she found her thoughts drawn once more to the early days when their hopes had been high and expectations even more unrealistic.

Chapter Three

They were married on a summer day just eight weeks from the day they met. It was a small gathering, as Julie wished, and Alex was happy to indulge her. His mother was disappointed and made no secret of it. She deplored the lack of pomp and circumstance and implied the haste with which they chose to marry would cause unpleasantness. In a daze of happiness and love, Julie was unmoved by Mrs. Brandt's dissatisfaction and, on her wedding day, moved down the aisle radiant in white veil and gown. Her only attendant was Ann Lawson. Julie's parents and younger brother and sister were there, but it was all a lovely dream, intermingled in her mind with candlelight and ivy and Alex's hand, warm and strong, holding her own.

For their honeymoon Alex secured the use of a secluded summer cabin from one of his friends. It was during that week that the depth of her husband's love was revealed to Julie. He tenderly led her through love's passages to a rich fulfillment such as she had never dreamed of. Shyly at first, then responding with growing confidence to his gentle guidance, she knew a joy and ecstasy beyond belief. She knew, too, that she pleased and delighted Alex with the artless abandon she offered him. They spent long hours with each other in the cabin, talking and loving.

It was decided that Julie should give up her job and become a full-time wife since Alex's work demanded quite a lot of entertaining and he was not always able to keep a regular schedule. If Julie felt a few qualms about leaving her job, she soon stifled them since she did not particularly feel satisfied in her job anyway. That had been the reason for taking the night classes. She had hoped to be able to work up into something interesting and worthwhile. However, compared to being Alex's wife, any job paled drastically.

Of course, her exact duties as his wife were a little vague since her mother-in-law had successfully persuaded Alex to continue on at the family residence. It was easily able to accommodate three people, she insisted, and this decision was the only one over which Julie felt real apprehension. Although nothing was ever said outwardly, she knew Mrs. Brandt did not like her and Julie would have been much more comfortable if she and Alex could have begun their married life in their own home. She determinedly pushed aside these fears and made every effort to settle into the impressive house.

Naturally there was a maid and cook, as it had been years since Mrs. Brandt had done any real work, so Julie found that she had lots of time on her hands. Any attempt on her part to contribute to the running of the house was firmly and politely refused as her mother-in-law had no intention of being usurped in her own territory. It soon became apparent that she considered the house hers, and Alex's of course, while Julie was made to feel an interloper.

None of this was ever evident to Alex and he remained happily unaware of the deteriorating relationship between his mother and his wife. Desperately anxious to please her husband, Julie concealed the growing fear that her mother-in-law would succeed in actually causing serious problems in her marriage if an opportunity ever presented itself.

One Monday morning when they had been married two months, Alex surprised her with a request that she plan dinner for the following Thursday. "I will be bringing some visitors home to discuss a business venture and it would be wise, I think, to combine business with dinner." He smiled at Julie. "You know some of them, but one or two will be strangers to you." She looked concerned for a moment and he added, "Don't worry, they will take one look at you and the evening will be a success!"

"I hope they aren't as silly as that," Julie returned wryly.

Alex laughed as his eyes ran over her lovingly, his thoughts apparent as his eyes narrowed, the lids lowering sensually.

Julie's flush was not lost on Mrs. Brandt, whose chill attitude toward Alex's indulgence to his wife was hard to ignore. How much more enjoyable our meals would be, Julie thought longingly, if only we could live alone. Incredibly, Alex still seemed unaware of any undercurrents between his wife and his mother.

Rising to leave, Alex named the guests he planned to invite for dinner and Julie was dismayed to learn that Angela Roswell would be among them. Mrs. Brandt had made it clear to Julie more than once, in Alex's absence, of course, that Angela was her choice of the perfect wife for Alex. She was well connected and had been in their circle since her teens. She had beauty and sophistication as well. Julie was always left with the uncomfortable feeling that she had few of these attributes and was just a little disappointing as Alex's wife. Angela was involved in her father's business, which provided an opportunity for her to see Alex often, and because of Mrs. Brandt's meaningful references to Angela and her obvious advantages, Julie felt slightly disquieted by his frequent contact with the other woman.

"I'll see you this evening, darling," he said as he shrugged into his coat. Kissing her lightly on the top of her head, he strode confidently from the room.

"Well," Julie said, rising quickly. "I'll get started on the menu and plans for Thursday."

Mrs. Brandt nodded coolly. "Of course, you must do what you please. But in the past when Alex entertained, I have used a very good caterer." She went on to name a prestigious firm. "I don't think Alex has ever had cause to complain," she continued, "but if you want to take the chance on doing this yourself . . ." Her voice trailed off, but the meaning was clear.

Julie drew a deep breath. "Thanks, Mrs. Brandt." She couldn't bring herself to address her mother-in-law in any other way, not that she had been requested to do so. "I think I will give it a try on my own. If I make a flop of it, I can always use the caterers next time." Privately she vowed to make the evening a memorable one or die. Gritting her teeth, she excused herself to begin planning.

On Thursday, a nervous and apprehensive Julie stood in the foyer with Alex greeting their guests. Her sparkle and vivacity was a facade which deceived everyone into thinking her a perfectly accom-

plished hostess while inside she was filled with a
trepidation which weakened her knees and brought a
moist film to her palms. Apprehensively she surveyed the guests. Angela had arrived, her sophistication a bright mantle of confidence. Her eyes, almost
midnight blue, fastened on Alex as her hands with
elongated perfectly manicured nails curled posses-
sively around his arm. What was Alex thinking?

It was that night that Julie met Robert Courtney.
Feeling a slight touch at her elbow, she looked up
into the eyes of a man whom Alex had introduced
earlier in the evening. Julie tried to recall a bit of
information about him, but that he was in some way
connected with banking was all she remembered.

"I can certainly see why Alex has been keeping
you to himself," he smiled warmly into her face.
"He has practically disappeared for the past two
months."

Liking him instantly, Julie responded warmly.
"Thank you . . . at least I think that is a compliment," she said, noticing his empty glass. "Can I get
you another drink?"

They moved over to the bar and Julie began
mixing his drink.

"What do you do with yourself all day?" he asked
as if he was really interested.

"Actually," Julie smiled ruefully, "not much."

He looked thoughtfully at Mrs. Brandt who was
seated regally alongside two matronly women, wives
of businessmen whose exact occupations were vague
to Julie. "I imagine Alex's mother has things pretty
well in hand here."

Julie looked quickly at him, surprised at the
accuracy with which he interpreted the situation. "I

try to keep myself occupied," she returned lightly, afraid she might inadvertently reveal just how unsatisfactory her days really were.

After mixing his drink, she handed it to him. Raising it, he saluted her and tasting it, replied, "I have known Alex for a long time. He certainly deserves the best and it looks like he has found it." He paused, then continued. "I just hope he realizes what a prize he has." The admiration in his eyes was unmistakable.

Unsure of his meaning or what he was implying, if anything, Julie smiled noncommittally and, excusing herself, moved away.

The evening had been a success. It was the beginning of several evenings which she arranged and all went according to her carefully laid plans. Her mother-in-law continued to show no warmth or any sign of relaxing her attitude toward Julie. Alex worked long hours and the days dragged. She and Robert had become good friends and lunched together several times when Alex was tied up. It was purely platonic. Robert seemed to sense that her love for Alex was the biggest thing in her life. He also understood that she was lonely and unsure of her real place in Alex's life. Quite unintentionally she found herself revealing her fears about her mother-in-law; it was comforting to be able to share her apprehension with someone who appreciated the uncertainty of her situation. For Alex certainly did not. Astonishingly he remained oblivious of the strain pervading his home.

It was the cause of their first quarrel. One evening as they were preparing for bed, Alex remembered to cancel lunch with her for the following day. "I've just learned that an important client will be in Boston for a few hours and I will need to use my lunch hour to talk with him," he explained.

All at once, Julie was angry. "Alex, is it really necessary for you to spend so much of your time with clients?" she complained. "This makes about six times that you have had to cancel lunch or dinner or some other date with me. Is it going to be necessary to make a business appointment with my own husband before I can be assured of seeing him?"

Alex was stunned. He stared at her wordlessly for a moment. "I hadn't realized that you were feeling neglected," he drawled, reaching for her, still unaware of the anger she was having difficulty containing.

She shrugged away from him. "Just leave me alone! You only have time for me at night in our bedroom," she accused.

"What are you talking about!"

"I'm talking about us. I never see you or have your complete attention unless we're in bed."

"Don't be ridiculous, Julie."

"That's right," she raged. "Call me ridiculous. You act like you really don't know what I'm talking about."

"I *don't* know what you're talking about," Alex returned calmly.

Suddenly she realized that he truly didn't know. She looked at him in defeat. "Alex, what do you think I do when you go off to work in the mornings?"

"Are you trying to tell me you're bored with our marriage already?" Alex asked quietly.

She drew a deep ragged breath. "No, Alex," she

said tiredly, "How could I be bored with you? I never see you."

Alex began pacing the room. Clad only in pajama bottoms, his naked skin gleamed in the soft lamplight. He thrust his fingers through his hair. "I didn't realize you were feeling this way. Mother is here to keep you company during the day. Surely you didn't expect to be entertained while I was busy at my office, did you?" He stopped abruptly as if a thought had just occurred to him. "I don't want you to start working again, Julie. My work is too demanding to have you complicating our lives by joining the rat race, too."

"I need to feel useful, Alex." Julie tried to explain her feelings. "I have never lived such a pointless existence."

"You see your role as my wife pointless?" Alex questioned aggressively.

"I didn't mean that at all!" The denial sprang from her lips.

"Then just what did you mean?" His voice was quiet, almost menacing.

Julie swallowed with difficulty. She hadn't intended getting into a free-for-all and she suspected that in anger Alex could be very dangerous. Indeed, she feared that she was going to be given a demonstration any minute now.

She began again. "Alex, your mother has charge of the house . . ." Futilely she tried to think of a way to explain her feelings of inadequacy regarding her position in the house, or lack of position, she thought ruefully. Alex was looking impatient.

"Well?" he demanded.

Wearily, Julie shook her head. "Never mind, Alex. Just forget it." Then, remembering what started the whole thing, "And I'll make other plans for lunch tomorrow."

Frowning, Alex inquired, "What do you usually do for lunch?"

Not liking him to know how she avoided lunching with his mother if she could help it, she mentioned meeting Ann Lawson and other friends occasionally.

"Haven't you been lunching with Robert Courtney quite a bit?" Alex queried as if suddenly interested in a fact that had been insignificant until now.

"What's that supposed to mean?" Julie was defensive and beginning to get angry again.

"You tell me." The line of his jaw hardened as he directed a suspicious look at her. "All this talk about being bored and lonely may just be a smoke screen. Mother said he calls you pretty often."

A red haze rose before Julie's eyes as she realized what Alex was implying. "If you have something to say, Alex," she began hotly, "then come out and say it." She paused. "But it had better be good, because what you are suggesting is pretty rotten!" She faced him with arms straight down beside her, fingers clenched into tight fists. In her transparent nightgown her breasts were heaving with the force of her rage.

As if he became aware that he had inadvertently blundered in mentioning his mother, Alex hesitated. "Look, Julie, we are both saying some strong things tonight. Let's stop this before some real damage is done." He walked over to the window. Reaching up to rub the back of his neck wearily, "I will be home early from the office tomorrow evening if I can possibly manage it." He turned, looking tired. The lines around his mouth were deeply scored. When relaxed he had a full sensual lower lip, but now, tightlipped and unsmiling, he looked forbidding. Julie shivered as with premonition of something dreadful to come.

He was already in bed when she finished washing her face and preparing for the night. She slipped into her side of the bed and switched off the light. Long after Alex was breathing deeply and evenly, Julie lay silent, tears sliding from her eyes onto her pillow. They did not make love.

It was obvious that Mrs. Brandt's curiosity was aroused by the heavy atmosphere at the breakfast table the next morning. Although outwardly polite, neither Julie nor Alex spoke directly to each other and the teasing indulgence which he usually displayed was absent from Alex's manner. Julie was certain she sensed a smug satisfaction in her mother-in-law's attitude. Any friction between Alex and Julie would please her.

She smiled archly at her son. "I have taken the liberty of inviting a few friends for dinner next Friday evening." She looked uncertain for a moment, then plaintively, "I hope it will be alright with you both. Naturally, I intend for us all to be there." She then named her guests and Julie gasped indignantly as she realized her mother-in-law's intent. Her guests included Angela Roswell as well as Robert Courtney.

Rising precipitately from the table, Julie mumbled an excuse and escaped. She simply could not bear the smugness and barely concealed hostility of her mother-in-law on top of her sore feelings as a result of her quarrel with Alex. Soon she heard the sound of the door as Alex slammed it shut and then the engine of his car as he left for work.

* * *

That dinner party would be remembered by Julie as one of the most horrible evenings of her life. Since their quarrel, she and Alex had been like strangers. She saw him briefly at breakfast where he ate sparingly, the newspaper alongside his plate, ignoring both Julie and his mother. He had not invited her for lunch, making it clear that business was taking most of his time. So completely was he immersed in his work that it was often late at night before he would arrive home, shrugging out of his coat wearily, and more often than not skipping dinner or replying tersely that he had grabbed a bite downtown in answer to her question.

Dressing for the dinner party was an ordeal. Julie dreaded the effort of smiling and pretending enjoyment she did not feel as the deterioration of her relationship with Alex rendered everything as tasteless as ashes in her mouth. There would be no pleasure for her in making charming conversation to Mrs. Brandt's guests, but try as she could, she was unable to think of a way to avoid the evening.

Robert, of course, sensed her unhappiness immediately. "What's wrong, Julie?" he asked directly when he had been in the house only ten minutes.

Julie laughed shakily. "Do I look that bad?"

"You never look bad," he returned, "but I know you very well, and you look as if you're going to splinter into a thousand pieces at the least provocation." His eyes studied her with concern.

"Then don't provoke me." Her laugh was brittle.

Robert looked over at Alex who was talking to Angela Roswell. "We haven't seen much of Angela lately," he commented pensively, watching as Angela, stunning in a clinging black dress which outlined her perfect figure, smiled seductively at Alex, her hand caressing his arm in a seemingly unconscious movement.

Bitterness welled up in Julie's throat. Her mother-in-law planned the evening so that Robert would even the numbers, allowing her to invite Angela. But Angela was really invited for Alex.

During dinner, Angela sparkled for Alex's benefit. Julie made an effort to seem uncaring, and thanks to Robert's moral support and sympathetic understanding, she managed to behave with charm and poise. When the evening was over and the last guest departed, she went straight to her room, thankful to be alone.

Feeling depressed and dispirited, she could hardly believe that only a few months ago she was optimistically anticipating her marriage to Alex, her heart full of love. She had honestly thought that being married to Alex would be heaven on earth and, sadly enough, she had believed that Alex felt the same. How wrong she had been.

Julie was so desolated by her thoughts that she burst into tears, falling face down onto the big bed that she and Alex had shared so joyously in the beginning, but which now contained the two of them each night, stiff and apart, strangers separated just as surely as if they were in different rooms.

After that night, a wary truce existed in their marriage. It took only a chance word to flare into a violent exchange. Their frequent quarrels made any hope of an amicable discussion of their problems impossible.

Most weekends Alex spent closeted in his small den, ostensibly to work, but Julie felt he simply wished to avoid her. Mrs. Brandt, content with matters as they were, said nothing. At least in front of Julie she said nothing. Several times, Julie was aware that her mother-in-law went into the den taking coffee or a snack to Alex and sometimes staying to talk a while. What they said or what they discussed remained a mystery to Julie. By now she was numb with pain and fear.

The end when it came was bitter and final. Several weeks had passed and in desperation Julie resolved to speak to Alex. It was ridiculous to remain silent, both of them absorbed in their own worlds. An open line of communication was an absolute necessity in a marriage. Well, she would surprise him at his office and they would talk.

A light snow was beginning to swirl as Julie left, pointing her car toward downtown Boston. Even at that early hour, driving was hazardous, so she was careful to pay strict attention in getting to Alex's office safely. Arriving, she parked her car in the area reserved for his firm and walked quickly into the building, shivering in the frigid air.

As she entered the foyer of the huge office complex, she stepped over to the elevators and once inside the tiny cubicle, pushed the button for the floor on which Alex's office was located. Her stomach was tight and her hands cold as she nervously rehearsed what she would say, how she would begin. How did one begin when one's whole happiness depended on the outcome of the conversation? Because Julie was convinced that this day her marriage to Alex hung in the balance and the result of their talk would mean a new beginning or the end.

Taking a deep breath, she moved out of the elevator. Down the corridor were rest rooms and knowing her hair was disheveled and flakes of snow were melting on her face and clothing, she headed for the ladies' room to tidy herself and make sure she looked her best.

After dawdling as long as possible, she knew she must get on with it. It was when she opened the door to step into the corridor that she saw Alex as he came out of his suite of offices. He was not alone. Angela Roswell was with him, holding onto his arm, smiling up at him, invitation in every sleek line.

Angela's voice floated down the hall, her husky tones provocative as she released the full extent of her charm on Alex. "I can't wait for tonight, Alex," she was purring. "Let's go somewhere cozy and quiet . . ."

Rising nausea threatened to overwhelm Julie. Quickly, she stepped back into the ladies' room, stumbling to the lavatory. It took all her control to keep from actually retching as in her pain and shock she faced the bitter truth. It was clear now why Alex had been preoccupied. Of course he didn't have time to spend with Julie. All the long hours and missed dinners were suddenly explained.

Making a valiant effort to calm herself, Julie waited until she felt certain Alex had gone; then she went out into the corridor and headed for the elevator. Once inside, she was rushed at sickening speed downward. Several public telephones were along the walls in the foyer of the building. Closing herself into one of the booths, she tremblingly dialed Ann's number which she had in the tiny address book. An empty, continuous ringing at the other end of the wire told her Ann was not at home. She replaced the receiver, shoulders drooping in hopelessness. What could Ann do anyway, she thought with despair. Surely this signaled the end of her marriage and the thought of the loneliness and emptiness ahead of her could hardly be borne.

She stumbled out into the street, the cold air hardly registering in her confused and reeling brain. Heading for her car, she opened the door and slid heavily behind the wheel. When she was at last driving, she realized she was near the art museum and impulsively turned into the drive. Once inside she wandered through the quiet halls seeing very little but strangely comforted by the beauty and grace of the art treasures displayed. Hours later she left, her steps dragging down the length of the marble steps and on to her car. It was still snowing intermittently, she thought dully.

The phone was ringing as she entered the house. It was Robert. The warmth of genuine pleasure in his voice comforted her bruised spirit and she gratefully agreed to go with him when he suggested dinner. He must have sensed the unhappiness and unspoken appeal in her voice as he arranged to pick her up at six o'clock. Tactfully he did not mention Alex.

Nothing would keep her indoors tonight waiting for Alex who just might or might not decide to check in at his own home, she vowed fiercely. In a mixture of defiance and misery, she headed upstairs.

She was ready when Robert called for her. Alex had not returned. She did not inform her mother-in-law where she was going nor did she leave a message for Alex. Mrs. Brandt looked curiously at her and with a little frown inquired if she thought it would be wise to go out with the weather threatening as it was. Julie murmured something as the doorbell rang. Opening it to Robert, she sensed Mrs. Brandt's surprise. For a moment she seemed almost concerned. Julie was vague and anxious to leave. Snow was not falling although flakes swirled in flurries from time to time, floating in front of the headlights like drunken fireflies.

Wishing to leave the congestion of the city behind, and in her somber mood, Julie suggested they dine at a restaurant along the coast a little north of Boston, just out of the city. Robert acquiesced, sensing that she was practically devastated by whatever had prompted the uncharacteristic acceptance of his dinner invitation. Something in her manner as he spoke to her on the telephone had prompted him to suggest dinner. Her agitated and eager acceptance had revealed more than Julie realized.

At the restaurant, warm with candlelight and almost empty, when they had ordered Robert gently probed. "I suppose something serious has happened to give you that look, Julie." His quiet concern was balm to her battered senses. "I don't know what Alex has done, but he's the only person in the world who can bring that shattered look to your eyes." Gently he leaned over and drew his fingers down her cheek. "He must be a damn fool!" he said wonderingly.

"I think I'm the fool," Julie replied, her mouth trembling as she tried to find words to explain her extraordinary behavior in agreeing to come out with Robert in such weather and under the circumstances. And for what? Already she was regretting involving another person in her personal problems. The mess she and Alex found themselves in was of their own making and only she and Alex could work it out.

Their food arrived. However, it was almost impossible for Julie to swallow.

"Robert," she began apologetically. "I hope you

will forgive me for selfishly using our friendship."
She smiled ruefully, and pushing the chicken around
her plate, she shoved it aside completely. "You have
been such a good friend to me but I am not going to
take any further advantage of your good nature
tonight, or ever again, except to ask you to take me
back home." Earnestly, she continued. "Something
did happen today that upset me, but I see now that it
will have to be worked out between Alex and me and
involving you was a mistake."

He started to protest, but Julie plunged on. "No, I
mean it, Robert. When you called, I was just fed up
enough to grab at any chance to score off Alex. I
should not have done so and I do apologize." She
looked worriedly out the window as though suddenly
aware of the menacing quality of the thickly falling
snow. "I just hope we haven't become stranded in
this weather."

Reluctantly, Robert accepted her explanation and
they both stood. After paying the check, Robert
retrieved their coats. Once outside the full brunt of
the wind and snow hit them squarely, and with an
arm under her elbow to assist her, they made their
way to Robert's car. Astonishingly, in the time they
had been eating dinner the snow had fallen with a
vengeance. It would be precarious driving and Robert immediately seated Julie in the car and began to
ease out onto the street.

It was soon apparent that to attempt to stay on the
road under the conditions created by the wind and
snow would be more than foolish. It would be
dangerous.

Later, when Julie tried to explain to Alex, the
situation seemed ridiculous and far-fetched. She and

Robert were forced off the highway to shelter at a small inn where they had been lucky to even find rooms. The freak blizzard had downed power lines in the area where they stayed, but the power stayed on back at home where Alex waited to hear from Julie. Incredibly, they were only just across town, but in the conditions which existed because of the storm, they were trapped. The night passed slowly and most of the next day. When they were able to get back home they found an angry, hostile, unbelieving Alex. Bitter accusations were hurled back and forth between them. The scene was a bleak culmination of the past weeks of misunderstandings and grievances, both of them tossing words indiscriminately, weapons chosen to wound and tear. When it was over, there was nothing left of their marriage.

Julie immediately moved out, and with Ann Lawson's help and unquestioning sympathy, she located an apartment and started looking for work. Frank Peters was a friend of Julie's father and because of the recent pregnancy of one of his employees, she was hired as a secretary. She threw herself and all her energies into the work, finding it challenging and rewarding. She quickly progressed. The additional training at night school proved beneficial and there were other courses which she took to fill her evenings. Robert proved a steady friend and would have liked to deepen their relationship but Julie could feel nothing more than affection for him. She gradually stopped seeing him as much for his own sake to prevent him harboring any hope for more than friendship with her as for her own lack of interest in any male companionship.

After that final shattering scene with Alex and

even before she packed her clothes to leave the house, the only emotion she felt was a merciful numbness.

The consuming love she had felt for Alex and the searing joy in their marriage which had characterized her life as his wife were dead. During the months that followed when she did occasionally think of him, she felt a gentle regret but nothing like the anguish she had feared in the weeks preceding their separation. The promise of never-ending happiness had faded into the mists of yesterday.

Quelling feelings which had been resurrected by the train of her thoughts, Julie looked around blankly. It was a moment before she could fully orient herself. These tramps in the woods had afforded her a time to try to sort out the confusion caused by Alex's sudden return to her life. Looking around her at the evidence of spring's inevitable return, she felt the stirrings of new life within her own self and knew that no longer could she continue to bury her feelings behind a wall of indifference. Her response to Alex in the short time since he had returned proved that.

Chapter Four

It was with a sense of anticipation not unmixed with fear that Julie arrived at her office on Monday morning. Refreshed and strangely calmed after her weekend in the Maine woods, she resolved to greet Alex more or less as a friend. There was no need to make any more of it than that, she assured herself.

It became obvious that day she was going to deal with Wes Blakeney, Alex's staff assistant, rather than Alex himself. Julie, somewhat chagrined, sternly lectured herself on the folly of allowing herself to become too much aware of Alex once again in her life. Wes proved to be thorough and professional in his approach to the problems at Peters-Winton.

Returning to her apartment that evening, she prepared a light meal and ate it quickly, solitude not particularly soothing for some reason. She was standing at the sink washing what few dishes she had used when the doorbell rang loudly, the sound startling her and causing a momentary pang deep in her stomach. Catching up a towel she moved to the door drying her hands as she walked.

There was no sense of surprise when on opening the door, Alex's tall form was outlined in the door frame. In a white knit pullover shirt which accented his bronze skin and gray pants, he looked lean and virile.

"Aren't you going to invite me in?" His voice was deep-pitched and achingly familiar. Apparently at his ease leaning against the door frame, he smiled, his mouth tilted crookedly. Only his eyes remained alert, Julie noted. They were dark gray, almost black. Silently she stepped aside to allow him to enter.

"Have you had dinner?"

He looked around. One sweeping glance revealed that she was alone. "I just finished."

Walking stiffly toward the tiny kitchen, she placed the towel on a rack and snapped off the light. Alex was standing at the door, not having come any further into the room. For a moment she imagined he looked uncertain. His next words dispelled that impression.

"Did you miss me today?" he grinned wickedly.

"Did you expect me to?"

"It crossed my mind." He strolled over to her, his eyes assessing her worn plaid shirt and faded jeans. "Don't I recognize that shirt? Didn't we pick that up in P-town?" Casually, he referred to the artist colony located on Cape Cod where they had spent one never-to-be-forgotten weekend.

Blindly she turned away so that he could not witness her pain. "I'm surprised you remembered," she replied sharply.

"I remember everything."

She looked around, startled.

"You still look beautiful and sexy in jeans."

Julie's heart began to pound softly. He was standing much too close. Desperately, she searched for words to dispel the atmosphere he had created. "Have you seen Wes?" she asked brightly.

Laughing silently, Alex stepped backward and Julie relaxed a bit.

"Yes, I've seen Wes." He seemed to accept her attempt to divert him. "He is just as impressed with Frank's girl Friday as I am," he drawled.

She smiled stiffly. "He seems terribly competent as are all your staff." Is this really me sounding so prim and pompous, Julie wondered, a little crazily.

"We try," he murmured sarcastically.

"Was there something special you needed to see me about?" she asked pointedly.

"I did have a reason for coming over tonight, Julie." He was still standing in one spot. He laughed shortly. "Aren't you going to ask me to sit down?"

Dragging her gaze from the sight of his overwhelming maleness, she gestured toward an armchair. "I'm sorry," she murmured. "Take that chair."

Reaching out suddenly, he grasped her wrist and pulled her down onto the sofa with him.

Caught by surprise, Julie began to struggle, but he restrained her easily. "Relax, Julie, I just want to talk to you." His hands pressed her shoulders back against the cushions. "You weren't in any condition last Friday night with that headache," he explained. "I really need to discuss something important."

Her attention arrested, Julie had difficulty thinking clearly. He really had a most unsettling effect on her!

"What do you want, Alex?" she asked suspiciously.

"How about a drink?" Alex got up and headed

into the kitchen, snapping the light on familiarly as though he did so every day. Exasperated and puzzled by his erratic behavior, Julie was up immediately to follow him. Only as she entered the tiny area was she suddenly aware of the confined space and how completely Alex filled it. Stepping in front of him, she opened a cabinet which held her small liquor supply and took down one bottle, banging it on the counter.

"Really, Alex, I don't appreciate you coming here and throwing me around on the sofa, helping yourself to drinks." Nervously, she took refuge in anger. "If you have something to say, just come out with it," Sighing as a sudden thought struck her. "I suppose you want a divorce now."

Tensely, not looking at him, she waited for Alex's reply.

There was a glint of mockery in his face as he turned to her. "What's the matter? Do you begrudge your husband a drink?"

Was he going to ignore her question? "OK, Alex, fix yourself a drink." She reached for a glass, unwilling for him to know the distress and anxiety that discussing a divorce with him would cause. It was what she wanted, wasn't it? She had always known that some day it would be necessary to dissolve their marriage. *But not yet*, a voice deep inside her insisted. *Not yet.*

Holding his drink in one hand, Alex grasped her upper arm with his other hand. His fingers felt warm and firm as they guided her out of the kitchen and back onto the sofa. It was a relief to leave the small area where his aggressive maleness overwhelmed her shaky defenses. Only after they were seated side by side did he release her arm and then he took a long swallow of his drink, placed the glass on a small table and turned to face her so that she felt the warmth of his body bent slightly toward her.

She was aware of his leanly muscled frame and once more the power that emanated from him caused her to blanch inwardly. Swallowing thickly, she raised her eyes to his neck, strong and brown. Where the vee of his shirt was open, she saw the beginning of crisp dark hair. In her imagination, she recalled the feel of his chest under her hands as they caressed him, warm and vital, and she could hear the sensual animal sounds he made when he was aroused.

Thrusting away treacherous thoughts, she leaned away from Alex in panic, but he caught both her hands in his to stop her.

"Why are you afraid of me, Julie?" he asked in frowning concern. "I'm having a little trouble finding the right words to use, but there is no reason for you to shy away like a frightened bird," he declared shortly. "I'm not going to push myself on you again, either," he added flatly.

"Please, Alex," Julie managed weakly. "Why are you here?"

"There are some things that need to be said," he began, "about us." He saw her eyes widen in apprehension. "Why did you mention divorce just now?" He eyed her intently.

Julie licked her lips as she sought for a reply. "Why do you want to know?" she returned. "Is that what this is all about?"

"No. I just thought it might be what you wanted." When she made no answer to this, he continued. "It's difficult to know just how to tell you this, Julie." He released her hands and straightened up out of the sofa. Looking down at her, he uttered a frustrated sound. "I want you to come home with me."

She stared at him with incredulous eyes.

"I don't know why you're looking like that," he declared. "You are still married to me and my home is still your home."

Bewildered, Julie shook her head. "What are you up to, Alex?" she asked sharply. "You know I can never go back to your home again." And then added bitterly, "Your mother would never allow it."

"That's just it, Julie. My mother is ill." Alex looked at her directly then, his face grim. "She had a severe stroke very soon after you left. For a long time, it looked as though she would never be able to get around again." His eyes narrowed as though recalling past pain. "She did rally after several months and now gets around with some difficulty."

"I'm sorry, Alex." Julie's voice was husky with sympathy. "I didn't know. I had no idea." She knew how devoted Alex was to his mother and even though she and her mother-in-law had never been able to live together compatibly, she would never have wished the pain and suffering of a stroke on her.

"Yes. Well, now that she is better, she has been worrying about me," Alex said ruefully. "She dwells on the fact that we," his mouth twisted wryly, "are apart and that she contributed to the whole thing."

Julie gasped with astonishment. Never had she expected Mrs. Brandt to admit to any of the responsibility of the break-up of their marriage.

"I can't believe it." Julie was stunned.

"I have tried to reason with her and assured her over and over again that she was not responsible, but she keeps on insisting that she is to blame." His voice was taut with strain and it was with difficulty that he continued. "As a matter of fact, she told me some things that I never knew . . . never suspected. It's hard for me to believe that I could have been so blind to the problems you were coping with while I was so wrapped up in my work. Anyway, she has become obsessed with the idea that if you would agree to come back," he looked quickly at her, "just for a short while, that things might be better." He laughed shortly. "I think she plans to be on her best behavior."

When he had finished, Julie was speechless. Perhaps she imagined the tense stillness with which he held himself as he waited for her reply.

"I don't know what to say, Alex," she began haltingly. "Of course, I'm very sorry about your mother, but to even consider moving back to your house . . ."

"Didn't I make it clear that it would be a temporary thing?" Alex was remote, his features unreadable. "Naturally, we would have separate bedrooms." His voice was ironic.

"Separate bedrooms?" she echoed.

"Unless you prefer to share mine . . ." His voice trailed off suggestively.

Jumping up suddenly, Julie wrung her hands in agitation. "You can't be serious, Alex," she protested. "It's ridiculous to expect me to do something like this just to pacify your mother."

Alex smiled lazily, his eyes roving over her face and lingering on her mouth. "Perhaps you would consider it to pacify me?"

Flushing, Julie stared at him, her lips parted wordlessly.

"I swore I was going to behave tonight," Alex began thickly. "But you shouldn't look at me like that." He reached out and pulled her to him urgently, his mouth coming down to cover hers hungrily, insistently, as though long deprived of the taste of her. Weak and yielding, Julie responded to his need, her own senses clamoring for fulfillment. He was kissing her desperately and deeply and Julie reeled in pleasure so sweet that she was mindless to everything but Alex's mouth and hands and the sensations he created so effortlessly. Somehow her blouse became separated from her jeans and his hands tenderly stroked and caressed her bare back and shoulders. Only when he lowered his mouth to the swell of her breasts did Julie realize what was happening.

Dazed, she dragged herself from his arms, trembling all over. She buried her face in her hands. "Get out of here, Alex," she sobbed. Making a tremendous effort to gain control of herself, she raised her eyes to his and gave him a contemptuous look, her eyes bright with tears. "All right, so you still have the power to arouse me," she accused bitterly. "It was despicable of you to use that kind of tactic to get what you want." Dashing tears from her cheeks with the palms of her hands, she lifted her chin, desperately trying to maintain some kind of control.

Alex stiffened. His face was still flushed from the intensity of the desire which raged between them. One hand reached involuntarily for her, but when she pulled backward he dropped it and sighed wearily. "Look, Julie, no matter what I said right now, I don't think you would believe me." He raked his hands through his hair. "I just want you to think about coming back home with me, that's all. We'll talk about it another time." Reaching the door, he turned back. "I'll see you tomorrow."

Julie prepared for bed in a daze. She was in no condition to think clearly about anything that Alex had said. She was still reeling from the aftermath of emotions he had aroused once again. That he would make such a fantastic request and then make love to her in order to lessen any resistance she might have offered sickened her. *And I'm not going to allow him to make me feel guilty about his mother either*, she vowed angrily. Of course, she did feel some compassion for the woman who had prided herself upon her strength and capability, Julie conceded reluctantly.

Once in bed, she turned out the light but lay with wide eyes. If only she knew how Alex felt about her personally. Illogically the idea of divorce was strangely repugnant to her. Although she had not actively sought a lawyer and actually begun the proceedings for the ultimate dissolution of their marriage, Julie had always assumed in the back of her mind that one day she would do so. However, Alex's return and the undeniable shock to her carefully constructed defenses could not be ignored no matter how firmly Julie insisted to herself that she was indifferent.

It was useless to try to sleep with the weight of her thoughts depressing her. Anxiously she pressed her hands against her middle which churned as though she had just run a race. Flinging back the bedclothes, Julie sat up and turned the bedside light on. Her clock showed the time as three in the morning. She left her bed and went into the kitchen, wearily lifting the weight of her hair off the back of her neck and stretching her spine to relieve the tension in her back. A cup of hot chocolate might be tranquilizing.

She fixed the drink and sipped the steaming liquid cautiously. After a few moments, she poured out the remaining liquid and rinsed the cup. She wandered back into the bedroom, resisting the urge to dwell any more on disquieting thoughts regarding Alex and her marriage. Fatigue overwhelmed her.

Her head ached with the intensity of her thoughts and the confusion of her emotions. Not to be discounted was a tiny flicker of hope, or anticipation, she didn't know which, that glimmered inside when she thought of being near Alex every day. It would be good, she told herself cautiously, to dispel some of the hostility between them. Finally, with these troubled thoughts a jumble in her head, Julie slipped into a restless sleep.

Alex was impatiently waiting for Julie when she arrived at her office the next day.

"Good morning." He greeted her with just the right shade of politeness and professionalism. Nothing in his manner hinted at anything more. In fact, it was difficult for Julie to believe that this cool, poised businessman could be the same person whose passionate assault the night before had briefly lowered her defenses and revealed them both for a moment as a man and a woman transcending their differences in mutual desire.

She drew a deep breath and taking her cue from him returned his greeting coolly. Aware that Candy was watching them with more than ordinary interest, Julie led the way into her office. With a mocking smile, Alex followed her, closing the door behind him.

"Wouldn't it interest your secretary to know our real relationship?" he remarked wickedly. The mockery in his voice was just what she needed to stiffen her determination not to allow him to rile her on her own territory.

"Surely you don't intend to pretend that you want things to be any other way," she intoned with heavy sarcasm. "From the first moment you appeared here you have shown no inclination to acknowledge our real relationship," Julie accused with emphasis on the last two words.

"Our real relationship!" His voice was harsh. "What the hell do you mean by accusing me of denying our real relationship! I'm taking my cues from you, Miss Julie Dunaway." His eyes were black with the force of his rage. "You have the nerve to accuse me when you have denied our marriage by going so far as to resume your maiden name!"

Julie felt her face flush. Under his scathing attack, the guilt she had always felt at denying Alex's name surfaced once again.

"How do you think I felt when you left?" he snarled. "You put me so completely out of your life that you didn't even bother to furnish me with a forwarding address!" Each contemptuous word hit Julie like a sharp knife, slicing the fragile fabric of her control. In spite of herself, Julie blanched a little in the face of Alex's unbridled feelings.

Moving nervously, she edged around behind her desk while Alex flicked out a notebook from the inside of his jacket and sat down. Julie had the distinct impression that he had drawn a mental line separating anything personal from the business of the day. That she was the "anything" caused her to wince inside, but she lifted her chin imperceptibly and prepared herself for whatever he planned next.

"Wes Blakeney had some interesting results from inquiries he made yesterday in the contracts department." Alex's attention was fully on the notes in his hand.

"Contracts department?" she echoed vaguely.

"Yes. Apparently bid packages and contracts are a combined function falling under John Fisher's jurisdiction."

"Bid packages?"

"For God's sake, Julie!" Alex exploded. "Are you going to repeat everything I say?"

"I'm sorry. I don't quite follow what you're suggesting."

"I'm not suggesting anything." Alex was impatient. "But these two functions are Fisher's responsibility, aren't they?"

"Yes. Yes, they are."

"OK. I need some more information . . . Some specifics if you can furnish them. If not, you will need to point me in the right direction."

"What do you need to know?" Julie's interest and attention were centered fully now on what Alex was talking about. For the time being, her lacerated feelings were thrust into the background.

Once again Julie was caught up in the sheer magnetism of Alex's personality. Most of her day was spent dealing with facts and figures concerning John Fisher's department. Fisher himself proved to be extremely uncooperative, even obstructive. Puzzled, Julie commented as much to Alex.

"I can't understand Fisher's attitude. He thinks of dozens of reasons why he can't furnish you with the material which you've requested." Her face mirrored her perplexity. "Mr. Peters would be very irritated to learn that he is not cooperating with you, Alex."

They were seated in a small coffee shop on the ground floor of the office building.

Alex sipped thoughtfully from a steaming mug. "You've done what Frank asked you to do in assisting me, Julie. Leave Fisher to me. I'll handle it from here on out."

He seemed preoccupied, but Julie knew him well enough to accept that he meant exactly what he said. He would take it from there. Since the angry exchange between them this morning, there had been no other harsh words. Once Alex slipped into his professional role, as Julie referred to it in her mind, he put aside all personal feelings and they worked amicably and well together. As a matter of fact, they worked together beautifully. She seemed to sense the trend of his thoughts and was particularly helpful because of that sensitivity. She knew that he valued her capability at her job. She was surprised at the pleasure his high regard brought her.

Once more her thoughts swung to Alex's request that she move back to his home temporarily. She knew him well enough to know that he would not accept her refusal as final. He was determined and skillful in getting what he wanted. It was frightening to know that he wielded such power over her. She feared that even the strongest resolutions would fade when he began to assert his will.

Perhaps that was one of the things wrong with their marriage. She had been so in love with Alex, so ready to capitulate to his will. Had she asserted herself more, demanded that they have a home of their own away from his mother, that he make more of a place for her, his wife, in his life, perhaps things would have turned out better.

Oh, it was all so hopeless, she agonized. It was too late—all water under the bridge. Alex would dearly love to choke her now—she recalled the morning's scene—rather than make love to her. Scolding herself fiercely, Julie returned to an awareness of her surroundings. Suddenly she looked across the table to find Alex watching her closely, a faint smile in his eyes.

"You were a million miles away," he teased. "What were you thinking about?" His smile faded. Abruptly he asked, "Were you considering what we talked about last night?"

Julie flushed at the accuracy of his guess. "What makes you think that?" she stalled.

"Well, were you?" He ignored her question.

"In a way," she admitted. "Did you really mean it, Alex?"

He studied her enigmatically. "I wouldn't have brought it up if I hadn't meant it. My mother is preoccupied with guilt over the failure of our marriage. Whether it's true or not, she feels it was in some way her fault. If you could bring yourself to come back for a little while . . ." Julie started to interrupt.

"Let me finish," Alex stopped her. "If you would come back for a little while it would mean a lot to me." He laughed ruefully.

Julie's heart sank. Inexplicably, the idea of going home with Alex appealed to her strongly but she was reluctant to examine the reasons too closely. Any contact with Alex was fraught with too many unknown quantities and it would be wise to proceed cautiously.

He was looking at her expectantly.

"Don't you think it would be . . ." she paused

awkwardly, ". . . difficult for us to live in the same house without . . ." She floundered helplessly. "Well, you know how you behaved in my apartment . . . the last two times you were there!" she accused him.

Alex smiled grimly. "It means a lot to me for you to do this, Julie." He seemed to search for words. "I can't deny that it's difficult for me to keep my hands off you." He slid a sensual look at her. "There has always been a terrific attraction between us, you know that." There was a rueful twist to his mouth. "But as you seem more than able to discourage me, I don't see the problem." Finishing his coffee, Alex stood. Effectively silenced, Julie followed him out.

As they waited for the elevator to carry them back to the upper offices, Julie sensed his regard, his lazy glance sliced downward, capturing her own contemplative study. His sensual mouth softened and she felt her resistance begin to lessen.

"Will you come with me tonight, Julie?"

Weakly she began a negative shake of her head even as her natural inclination was to comply.

"I . . . I don't think . . ." She licked her lips nervously, still immobilized by his dark gaze.

"Don't think, Julie." The elevator slid open in front of them, but Alex placed a restraining hand on her arm, hard and brown, but gently halting. His look impaled her while she made a futile effort to refuse him. She drew a long, shaky breath and nodded in capitulation. She felt the tension snap as Alex relaxed and drew her against him into the elevator. The door closed on them.

That evening, the drive to Alex's house was accomplished for the most part in silence. Dozens of thoughts tumbled around in Julie's head, but she couldn't bring herself to voice them and begin something that could very well be painful and futile. To play it by ear seemed the best course until she could sort it all out. Nervously she wondered at the reception she would receive. Certainly Mrs. Brandt had some purpose in engineering this meeting, but that it could be a reconciliation was so incredible to Julie that she was unable to credit that possibility.

They were nearing the affluent neighborhood where Alex had lived since childhood. Neat, well-kept lawns flanked impressive residences, each one tucked discreetly back from the street with only a tantalizing flash of window or weathered brick here and there to hint at the lavish lifestyle existing within. Remembering the awe with which she entered Alex's house for the first time, a small smile tugged at her mouth, not unmixed with regret.

"Something funny?" Alex's voice interrupted the bittersweet reverie.

Julie blinked. "Nothing. Just thinking." Her hands twisted nervously in her lap.

"Don't be nervous, Julie. Believe me," he continued with quiet emphasis, "my mother is anxious for this meeting and in her present state you will be more than able to cope with anything she might do or say."

"Were you aware that there was a time when I wasn't able to cope with your mother?" Julie's voice rang with bitterness.

He drew a long breath. "At the time, no." He shook his head in disbelief. "Although knowing what I now know, it must seem incredible that I could have been so blind."

Julie mulled this over thoughtfully. Perhaps she had been too discreet and too conscientious in her efforts to hide from her husband any incompatibility with her mother-in-law.

Alex's voice once again interrupted her thoughts.

"It may be difficult for you to show any affection for my mother, Julie, but if you have any compassion at all, please be kind to her." He frowned. "I'm not sure what she has planned. Just humor her a bit."

"I hope I've made it clear to you, Alex, that I'm just making this visit out of respect for your mother in her illness. I don't intend it to be construed as agreeing to return to your house to live," Julie stressed.

"Right. Like I said, just humor her in this."

"She will certainly be able to see that we aren't the usual reunited lovers," Julie continued doggedly. "So I don't think there is very much point in all this." She felt his sharp glance.

"You won't say anything to upset her, will you?"

"Of course not, but I don't think I can say anything that will raise her hopes, either. It's ridiculous to think that I could consider moving back into that house!" Agitatedly, she twisted the strap of her handbag.

"Why is it ridiculous?" He eyed her implacably.

"You know why! We can't just pretend that because your mother has suddenly become ill . . ."

"It isn't sudden. She's been ill for a year."

Julie continued as if he hadn't spoken. "That the reasons for our . . ." She struggled on desperately. ". . . the terrible things that caused our breakup . . ." Now her lips were trembling uncontrollably. "We can't just pretend all that didn't happen."

"What terrible things?"

"Really, Alex! You know what I'm talking about."

Staring ahead he stated calmly, "I know that our marriage began as a beautiful thing." Her breath caught sharply at his words. "And that we foolishly allowed other people to influence our feelings for each other." He turned to her with a direct look. "We both behaved in a way that jeopardized what could have been the beginning of a marriage that would have lasted forever."

"What are you trying to say, Alex?"

"Only that we started off with something good and unfortunately we got sidetracked somewhere along the way. Perhaps what we had is destroyed, but perhaps, also, it isn't." They were only a few moments from his house now, but Julie was unaware of this as she vainly tried to analyze what Alex was saying. Was he suggesting that the accusations hurled in anger and her own suspicions regarding Alex and Angela should simply be forgotten, dismissed as though they had never existed? In confusion, Julie began to speak, to try to discover exactly what he was suggesting, but just at that moment, Alex swung the car into a long driveway and she saw with surprise that they had arrived.

In the anxiety of the drive and the turmoil caused by Alex's strange remarks, her precarious self-control had suffered badly. Now, confronting the place where she and Alex had begun their marriage, she made a desperate attempt toward self-possession. It was vital that she present a calm facade to Mrs. Brandt.

Chapter Five

"Mother! We're home," Alex called.

Instantly, so that Julie knew she had been hovering near the foyer, Mrs. Brandt appeared. The sight of her mother-in-law shocked Julie even though she had expected some alteration in the forceful woman. Still, the ravaged face with one side pitifully drawn in the classic look of the stroke victim caught Julie unawares. Alex's telling her of Mrs. Brandt's condition had not prepared her adequately for the change in the older woman's appearance, Julie realized. Unaccountably, she had expected the same indomitable spirit, but meeting the wary and yet hopeful look in her eyes, it was more than apparent that there was no hostility left.

With the generosity of spirit that Alex had known she possessed, Julie leaned forward impulsively and kissed her mother-in-law on her pale cheek. "Hello, Mrs. Brandt," she whispered softly.

Struggling slightly, but with a gesture reminiscent of her former dignity, Mrs. Brandt inclined her head regally and reached for one of Julie's hands. She spoke haltingly.

"I hoped you would come, Julie. Thank you," she said simply.

Uncertainly, Julie followed as Alex assisted his mother, who moved awkwardly with an invalid's walker, into the gracious living room. In a rush of feeling Julie looked around, sensing as ever the serenity of her favorite room when she had lived here. Often she would seek its solitude in her own pain and isolation. The traditional sofa was cut velvet in coffee and blue stripes. Matching blue chairs flanking one side at a corner were placed at a right angle to the sofa. The cream carpet and walls combined with the overall effect to create a peaceful, quiet elegance. Placed here and there were small antique tables and curios.

Alex was gently assisting his mother to sit down.

There was no evidence of the coldness to which Julie was accustomed in her eyes when she turned eagerly to Julie.

"It's so good of you to agree to visit with me, Julie," she began haltingly, the effects of the incapacitating stroke causing her to grope to express herself. "It shames me more than I can ever say to know that I failed to welcome you to Alex's home when you were first married . . ."

Julie, distressed at such plain speaking, spoke impulsively.

"Oh, Mrs. Brandt, please don't talk like that. It isn't necessary, I assure you."

Her mother-in-law smiled crookedly. "On the contrary, my dear, it is necessary." Turning to Alex, "Please go and let Sarah know that you have arrived, Alex. She is waiting to serve us coffee." Hesitating only briefly, with an unreadable look in Julie's direction, he turned and left the room.

Mrs. Brandt gestured apologetically. "I suppose that was a bit obvious, Julie, but I did want to have you to myself for a moment." Julie tensed in sudden apprehension, but Mrs. Brandt continued. "Alex tells me that you were not aware that I had suffered a stroke just at the time that you two separated." Her gaze was clear and direct. The possibility of any devious intent on the part of her mother-in-law was diminished in the straightforwardness of her manner. "I believe that if I had not taken ill at just that time, Alex would have followed you immediately, Julie, and within a few days you would have returned home." She shook her head. "Sadly, he was torn between his duty to a sick mother and a wife whose reasons for leaving were almost a complete mystery to him."

Surprise rendered Julie silent.

"Oh, yes. I am aware that Alex did not know of the difficulties you faced when you were left alone in this house with me." Pain flickered across the strained features. "Any excuse I can offer would sound pitiful compared to the damage that I have done, my dear, but I can only say that I was frightened of being displaced, of finding myself having to live alone and, most of all, having to share Alex's love with another woman."

She smiled faintly. "Can you imagine my feelings, Julie, when I first saw you and Alex together?"

Julie murmured inarticulately.

"Alex adored you and I knew it at first glance. Because of that, you represented more of a threat than Angela would ever have done. She would have made Alex a suitable wife," emphasizing the word with a rueful twist of her mouth. "I sensed he would never feel for her the depth of love he felt for you."

Julie felt a pang at the private glimpse she was being given of a woman who once would never have revealed any hint of vulnerability to her daughter-in-law.

"I deluded myself into believing Alex found Angela attractive." Mrs. Brandt leaned forward slightly, fixing Julie with a compelling look. "You see, Julie, in my fear, I rationalized that I knew what would be best for my son, while what I was doing was manipulating my son's life according to what would be best for me."

Julie could bear no more. "Mrs. Brandt, please don't distress yourself by saying all these things. All that is in the past and absolutely no good can come of bringing it up again." In her agitation, Julie had jumped up and walked over to the window, staring unseeing out onto the beautifully landscaped grounds which had afforded her so much pleasure at one time.

"I certainly hope you don't mean that, Julie," her mother-in-law protested with a weak laugh. "I'm counting on something good happening from . . ." she gestured vaguely with a trembling arm, "all this. Both Alex and you have suffered because of me . . . No, it's true," she insisted when Julie would have interrupted once again. "Alex has been like a man half alive and I can do no less than attempt to put right what I, in my selfishness, did wrong." Seeing that nothing was going to prevent Mrs. Brandt from saying what was on her mind, Julie looked around wildly for Alex and the promised coffee. To her dismay, there was no sign of either.

Mrs. Brandt leaned over and gestured toward the sofa nearest her. "Sit down, dear, and let me finish." Resignedly, Julie subsided into the deep cushions.

"I know that you have managed beautifully on

your own, Julie, for the past two years that you have been away from Alex. I know that you have a job and that you have been very successful." She met her daughter-in-law's eyes directly. "Would you please consider coming back here to live . . ." Julie made an inarticulate sound. "Wait and let me finish, please," Mrs. Brandt was saying. "If you would agree to return, just for a while, Julie, perhaps things could be worked out between you and Alex. Naturally you would retain your job, but live here in your home. I have given this much thought and I'm convinced that if both of you will try to give your marriage one more chance, it will all work out." The strain of expressing herself was obvious as Mrs. Brandt leaned back weakly. "I promise you that I will never interfere in your marriage again," she whispered.

The intensity of her words moved Julie deeply. Suddenly she realized that she longed to make peace with Alex, to be his wife in every sense of the word again. But the damage done by each of them, shouting accusations, hurling recriminations, how could they ever heal the wounds?

Oh, this is blackmail, Julie thought agitatedly, moral blackmail. And Alex was fully conscious of the impossible predicament in which his bringing her to the house today placed her.

"Miss Julie, how very nice to see you." The voice of Sarah, elderly housemaid for the Brandts for years, reached Julie through the turmoil of her thoughts. She had been fond of Sarah and had sensed in the kind-hearted woman a sympathetic understanding of her problems during the months she had lived in this house.

Making a strong effort to conceal her thoughts, Julie smiled at Sarah and rose to take her hand in greeting. Alex, bringing up the rear, carried the coffee tray, attractively laid out with a wide variety of food suitable to accompany coffee or tea. Her mother-in-law invariably preferred afternoon tea and in the past Julie's preference for coffee had been made to seem less than gracious. Things certainly were different, Julie thought wryly, and was immediately ashamed of herself. Mrs. Brandt's efforts to please her and to persuade her to return to Alex's home were evidently sincere. Julie resolved in that moment to respond sincerely. Within reason, she amended cautiously.

The look Alex directed her way was searching and intent. Unwilling for him to detect her utter confusion and uncertainty, she avoided his eyes, accepting the cup proffered by Sarah and sinking once more onto the sofa.

"Julie and I have had a very nice conversation," Mrs. Brandt was saying. "I'm afraid I have surprised her, Alex, but I hope that when she has some time to consider my plea, she will be inclined to agree that what I have suggested has possibilities."

"She looks upset," Alex said flatly, his words calculated to bring her eyes around, wide and golden, to glare into his. As ever, it was impossible to read his thoughts. "Just exactly what have you been suggesting, Mother?" He was still watching Julie.

The nerve of him, Julie thought angrily. He acts as though he has no idea that I have been subjected to a painful emotional scene. Seeing Alex daily would be hell. Of course, his mother couldn't know how difficult it would be to live with him pretending that their marriage was normal on the surface while in reality it would be the biggest farce of all time, she concluded reluctantly.

Still refusing to look at Alex, she became aware of the tension and lack of color in her mother-in-law's features. Instinctively, Julie knew that the difficulty of voicing her imagined guilt and pleading with her daughter-in-law to come back had taken its toll of Mrs. Brandt's frail strength, and Julie cast a worried look in her direction. Then, to Alex, "Your mother is very tired, Alex," she said stiffly. "Why don't you help her to her room?"

Immediately, Alex turned aside to place his cup on a small table and went to his mother. He gently helped her up, placing her walker within her grasp. She protested that she was perfectly able to visit a while longer, but he firmly ushered her out of the room, calling to Julie over his shoulder. "Finish your coffee. I won't be a minute."

Left alone, Julie rose from the sofa and carried her coffee to the window. Looking out she deliberately concentrated on the peaceful view. After a few moments, she felt calm and turned back to find Alex propped against the door jamb watching her intently. Imperceptibly her chin rose.

His words surprised her. "Do you still find pleasure in looking out at these grounds?" His mouth quirked in amusement.

Caught off guard, she took a moment to readjust her thoughts. She threw him a quick look, uncertain whether or not he was being sarcastic at her expense. Seeing that he wasn't, she turned back to the window with a soft smile, unaware of the slim and graceful line of her back. "Yes, I do. I always found this particular spot beautiful and serene." Relieved to delay any painful discussion, Julie relaxed a little more. With a tingle, she felt Alex's presence next to her.

Pensively, he stood beside her staring out. "My father loved this view," he said. "If he had some troublesome case on his mind, he would stand just about here and puff on his pipe and stare out over the grounds. I've known him to spend most of an afternoon and evening doing that." He looked down at her. "You would have liked my father, Julie. You and he have a lot in common."

In surprise, Julie asked, "In what way?"

Alex narrowed his eyes as he considered. "Well, for one thing, he was an introspective person whose real thoughts and feelings were buried deep within." He paused and looked at her. "So are you, I found."

Julie started. She had always felt Alex could read her like an open book. Could it be possible he had been as uncertain about her as she herself had been about him? It was a new thought.

"You never mentioned your father very much. It was difficult for me to get a very clear picture of your life before I came into it." Julie's voice was soft and deep with remembered pain, recalling how she had longed to fathom Alex's feelings and needs during those brief months when she struggled to make a success of their marriage. Looking into his face, she saw a grimness there, a thinning of his mouth, and she noticed with surprise that his jaw was clenched as if his thoughts caused him pain. Sighing with regret, she was once more reminded how unfathomable her husband had always been.

Alex turned abruptly from the window, meeting her puzzled gaze. "What is my mother up to now?" he asked.

Taking a moment to form a reply, Julie began to ease over toward the sofa, needing to move away from his compelling closeness. Alex reached out a hand, curling it around her wrist, to stop her. "Don't go away from me now, Julie. It's a good time for us to talk."

Had he also been affected by shared memories a moment ago? she wondered. Maybe she hadn't completely imagined they had drawn close for a tiny while as they gazed out the window and he reminisced about his father. The possibility lightened her heart.

"I don't intend for Mother to intrude on my private life ever again," he stated grimly, "so whatever it is she is planning, I want to know all about it." His implacable gaze caught and held hers as surely as his strong hand held her wrist.

"Are you seriously telling me you aren't aware that your mother has practically made it impossible for me not to come back here at least for a temporary reconciliation?" Bitterly Julie emphasized the last two words.

Alex's eyes widened in surprise. Then, frowning, "What exactly are you saying?"

Julie took a deep breath. "Your mother has imagined that she contributed to our separation and has asked me to come back here temporarily to try and salvage something from the ashes." Julie's mouth trembled. "She apologized very sincerely, Alex." Biting her lower lip, Julie turned aside, tugging at her wrist still imprisoned within his hand. "She understands that I will not want to give up my job and has promised that she will not do anything to cause me any awkwardness while I am here."

Alex was silent. Julie turned suddenly. "The way she has gone about this, Alex, makes it almost impossible for me to refuse."

In her agitation, Julie did not see the light flare in Alex's eyes at her words.

"If I refuse to come, I'm afraid her condition will worsen or something." Vaguely she was aware that Alex had released her hand and was lighting a cigarette. She looked at him through the blue haze of smoke, attempting to read his expression and get some idea of his feelings.

"Would it really be a great imposition on you to agree to come here for a short time, Julie?" His quiet voice gave no hint of any emotion whatsoever.

She turned her back on him. God, how to answer? To live in the same house with Alex again and see him every day. Eat their meals together again. It was almost more than she could bear to think about. It would cost her dearly to conceal her real feelings under such intimate conditions.

"I assume by your silence that you don't agree." Alex's sarcastic comment cut through her chaotic thoughts. "Why can't you put yourself out just this once for an old lady who is genuinely trying to atone for what she feels is a mistake she has made against us?" he demanded bitingly. "It won't cost you a thing, I'll see to that. Your apartment lease will be taken care of and all you have to do is pretend to give it a try for three months. That should satisfy her." Viciously, he crushed out the half-smoked cigarette.

"Do you really think I have no more feelings than that?" Julie asked incredulously. "Can you honestly believe that all I'm thinking about in this ridiculous situation is my apartment lease?"

"Well, what are you thinking of?" he retorted.

"What about the strain of living with a conceited, arrogant selfish chauvinist like you?" she threw at him.

He grinned suddenly. "I never thought of myself as a chauvinist."

She stamped her foot impotently. "This is not funny, Alex!"

Schooling his features with an effort, he reached for both her hands and enfolded them warmly within his own. He looked down into her face. "Julie, if you do this to please my mother, I promise I will not act conceited, arrogant or selfish while you are here." He gave both her hands an admonishing shake. "And at the office I've never treated you chauvinistically. That's an unfair accusation," he teased.

Refusing to look at him, Julie stood quietly. How good it felt to have Alex holding her hands and making promises to her. Even if the next three months proved more painful than she could bear, it would be worth it just to pretend to be his wife again.

She knew she would have to give in.

The drive back to her apartment was accomplished in silence for the most part. Alex only spoke absently as they drove through the dark streets and Julie's thoughts were occupied with wondering how she had come to meekly accede to Alex's wishes once again and how to bear the next three months in close contact with the only man whose appeal was practically irresistible to her. Irrepressibly the humor of the situation struck her and she giggled a trifle hysterically.

Alex's head jerked around. "What's funny?"

"Nothing. Everything." She shrugged fatalistically. "We mustn't lose our sense of humor."

"Just keep that thought in mind and the next three months will be a piece of cake." The lines around his mouth deepened as he repressed a smile.

Inexplicably, Julie relaxed. She leaned her head back against the seat and felt the tense muscles of her shoulders and stomach relax as she mentally transferred the problems and worry of the plan over to Alex. Why not, she thought. He was certainly capable enough of bearing any amount of stress, so she may as well take advantage of it. Three months wasn't a very long time, and in the past two years Julie had struggled alone, shouldering all responsibilities for her survival which at times had been quite devastating. It would be heaven to lean against Alex's solid strength, let his determination and sheer maleness take over. She would only be along for the ride and afterward, she shrank inwardly at the thought, afterward she would pick up the threads and go on as before.

She felt Alex turn to her once again. "Willing to trust me a little to handle this, Julie?" His voice was warm and compelling in the darkness. Giving herself up to the feeling of the moment, she nodded in agreement.

"We'll begin moving your things after work tomorrow evening."

"So soon?"

"I can't see any point in delaying, can you?"

She made no reply.

"Right." He pulled in at the curb in front of her apartment building and she dazedly opened the car door. He came around to meet her at the sidewalk and together they walked up the steps and entered the brownstone. When she arrived at the door, she fumbled with the key and he pushed her hand aside impatiently. The door opened under his neat treatment. She braced herself for whatever came next, not sure that she could withstand any assault on her senses. But he guided her over the threshold, placed the key in her limp hand and closed the door with a quiet click. With a perverse feeling of being let down, she turned from the door, shed her jacket and headed for the bedroom. Moments later she crawled between the sheets, exhausted but strangely tranquil. She slept deeply.

The next morning Julie awoke with a tingle of pleased anticipation. For a moment she lay still and puzzled. Then with a suddenness that pierced slowly awakening senses she recalled that she would awaken the following morning once again in Alex's home. She flung the covers aside as if they were her own treacherous thoughts, refusing to consider again the folly of agreeing to Alex's irresistible persuasions, and headed for the bathroom. Under a warm shower, her tempestuous thoughts subsided somewhat and deliberately setting aside the obvious problems and complications which would beset her once she found herself living with her husband, she dressed carefully for work.

When she closed and locked the door of the apartment carefully behind her, she looked up to find Ann Lawson surveying her intently.

"Good morning," her friend greeted, smiling at Julie and eyeing her with more than casual interest.

"Isn't it a beautiful day!" Julie's wide smile provoked an answering gleam from Ann.

"Hold up a minute and I'll walk out to the street with you." Ann turned back and inserted a key into the lock to secure her own door. Straightening, she joined Julie and they fell into step together.

"Guess who I ran into in the hall last night," Ann teased gently, sending a smiling but sharp glance at her friend.

Julie bent her head while studiously rummaging through her handbag. "Who?"

"Your husband."

"Oh."

With an exasperated laugh, Ann paused uncertainly. "Is everything OK, Julie?"

For a moment Julie was tempted to avoid discussing Alex's recent return to her life. For just a little while longer, she wanted to savor the secret joy which filled her heart whenever she thought of him, anticipated seeing him, even when the inevitable clashes happened. It was as if she had suddenly come alive again after drifting along for a long time just half-alive.

"Hey, wake up," Ann interrupted playfully.

Knowing that her friend's curiosity was sincere and motivated by concern for her, Julie considered how to explain her sudden change of attitude toward Alex. Although Ann did not know the particulars of those weeks when Julie's marriage finally ended, she did know that Julie had taken refuge in anger and bitterness against Alex and it must be puzzling to find a complete absence of any ill feeling against him on her part.

"Ann, Alex's firm has been retained by Mr. Peters to make a study of the situation at work," Julie began haltingly.

Ann's eyes widened. "What a coincidence!"

"Yes, well," Julie faltered, "I was pretty stunned myself, and when I was still reeling from seeing him again, Mr. Peters informed me that it would be my responsibility to assist Alex while he was at the office." Memories of that scene darkened Julie's eyes momentarily.

Ann frowned. "That still doesn't explain why Alex was here last night."

With flushed cheeks, Julie looked away awkwardly, chewing her lower lip as she sought for words. She drew a deep breath.

"Oh, Ann, so much has happened in the last two days, I hardly know how to explain."

Immediately, her friend's expression softened. "You certainly don't have to explain anything to me, Julie. Your relationship with Alex is absolutely none of my business and I don't think I need to tell you that I wasn't attempting to pry."

"I know that." Julie smiled a little shakily. "You were such a good friend to me when I needed one that it never occurred to me to consider your concern as anything but sincere." She looked away thoughtfully. "I'm not sure I can explain my actions right now, Ann. Alex's mother apparently suffered a stroke just at the time that he and I separated. She has worried about our situation to such an extent that Alex feels it would be very helpful to her condition if we were to live together again." She swallowed painfully. "At least try to reconcile our differences for her sake."

"For her sake!" Ann repeated incredulously.

"Actually, yes. You know, relieve her of the strain of worry and guilt so that in time she may regain her health."

"And then you'll be off the hook, huh?" At Ann's sarcasm, Julie winced.

"It's not really that bad," she replied anxiously.

"Mrs. Brandt has changed, Ann, since her stroke. She apologized for not having welcomed me when Alex and I first married and I believe she was truly sincere when she asked us to give our marriage another try."

Head tilted to one side thoughtfully, Ann studied Julie's face. "And how does Alex feel about this reconciliation?" There had been a slight pause before the last word.

A worried look entered Julie's eyes. "That's something I can't answer. He is determined to make me come back but I don't know his real reasons," she murmured tremulously.

"When are you going?"

"Would you believe—tonight?" she joked wryly.

Speechless, Ann gasped, "You've got to be kidding!"

"As Alex said, there isn't any reason to delay, is there?" With a kind of desperation, Julie gestured helplessly.

Ann's penetrating look lingered for long moments on her face. She moved uncomfortably, feeling vulnerable and exposed under her friend's intense scrutiny. Was it possible that her feelings were written on her face for the world to see? How humiliating if her pathetic hopes were revealed for the pitiful things they were.

Strangely enough, Ann's regard relaxed somewhat and in a more gentle tone inquired, "And what happens when Mrs. Brandt does improve and your presence is no longer necessary for her welfare?"

Cringing from the pain of a possibility that had already occurred to Julie, she lifted her chin slightly. "Naturally, we'll go our separate ways. I'm retaining the lease to my apartment and of course I intend to stay in my job."

Ann spoke consideringly. "I always thought you and Alex were well suited, Julie. Maybe this will be a second chance for you both to make your marriage succeed. After all, neither of you opted for divorce."

"When we first separated, I expected every day to get a letter from Alex's attorney," Julie mused. "I never did."

Chapter Six

When Julie arrived at her office, John Fisher was waiting for her, fuming impatiently. Lately Julie dreaded any contact with him because of his unexplained hostility toward her. At a loss as to why he should be angry with her, she had steered clear of him when possible. But, drawing a deep breath, she braced for an unavoidable confrontation.

She shot him a quick stiff smile. "What can I do for you so early this morning, John?"

He frowned, ignoring any semblance of friendliness. "I want to know what you've been telling Alex Brandt about my department that is causing him to concentrate his sneaky efforts in my business!"

Julie gasped in astonishment.

"Don't give me that phoney innocent act!" he sneered. Without giving her a chance to reply, he continued, his voice harsh and raised angrily. "Brandt and his henchmen have spent most of their time nosing around my shop. When I asked them what the hell they're looking for, all they do is put me off!" He glared at her fiercely. "I want to know now what you have told them and why they're harassing me."

Refusing to be intimidated, Julie replied calmly,

"I don't know what they are looking for in your department, John, and you can be assured that I have told them nothing about your duties that they did not ask me directly."

His eyes thinned ominously as he threatened, "If you think I'm going to take this lying down, you have another thought coming! There are ways of handling uppity women like you and if you know what's good for you, you'll back off right now!"

"Or you'll do what?" Alex's quiet voice directly behind him startled Fisher momentarily, but his anger was still directed at Julie and he ignored Alex.

"He sure appeared on the spot at the right time," Fisher sneered. "Did you two come in together and he was just parking the car?"

In the deadly silence that followed, Julie watched in speechless horror as Alex moved to directly face Fisher, whose rage cooled somewhat when he encountered the implacable expression glinting from Alex's eyes. Involuntarily, he stepped backward but Alex reached out calmly and caught both lapels in one hand. Julie could see the knuckles whiten at the strength used to grasp the material.

"I'm only going to say this once, Fisher." Alex spoke softly, ominously. "If you ever speak to my wife again in that tone, or if you ever threaten her in any way again, I will personally break you into little pieces."

He released the viselike hold on Fisher's suit with a vicious little twist and stepped back as if close proximity was distasteful. Every vestige of color was drained from Fisher's face as he cast one more baleful glance in Julie's direction and disappeared out of the door.

Weakly Julie leaned against her desk. Alex moved

up to her and pulled her against his chest and began to rub her back and shoulders with both his hands comfortingly. She could feel his heart thudding rhythmically and the sound was ordinary and calming to her shattered senses. She felt brutalized and shocked by the unexpected venom of Fisher's attack.

Alex's hand moved up to smooth the back of her neck, kneading the taut muscles gently. "I'm sorry you had to put up with that kind of abuse, Julie." His voice hardened. "Especially since you don't know what the hell he's talking about."

Julie looked up, her eyes puzzled. "What's going on, Alex? Whatever it is, it must be something John feels threatens him personally. He was absolutely enraged." She paused thoughtfully. "And, if I'm not mistaken, he is badly shaken." Suddenly conscious of where she was, Julie hastily pulled away from the undeniable comfort of Alex's arms.

"Alex! Do you realize that you called me your wife just now?"

"What of it? Aren't you my wife?" he replied coolly.

"You know what I mean!" she returned impatiently. "No one here was aware of that fact and now it will be all over the building in an hour. How are we going to explain it?"

"Personally, I'm not expecting anyone to question me about a matter that I consider no one's business but my own," her husband stated arrogantly, "but if someone does take it into his head to question me," he laughed unpleasantly, "I believe that I can adequately explain it."

Julie winced inwardly as she imagined a scene whereby some unfortunate individual foolishly dared to mention to Alex his marital status.

Then impatiently returning to the problem at hand, she stood suddenly, feeling the need to face Alex on a more equal basis. "Surely you realize that Mr. Peters will require some sort of explanation."

Alex remained unmoved. "Leave Frank to me."

Fixing him with a long stare, Julie sighed in resignation. "I don't suppose it can matter very much anyway. Everything is in such a muddle that I wonder if my life will ever straighten itself out again," she said wearily.

"If you're sure that you will be OK," he began, "I'll go along to Frank's office before Fisher has a chance to do his dirty work."

"I still don't know what's going on and why John felt justified in accusing me of telling tales out of school," Julie said worriedly. "Will you come back after seeing Mr. Peters?"

With his hand on the doorknob, Alex turned back. "There is nothing for you to be concerned about, Julie. As I said before, you furnished me with the facts and figures as requested and now it is my job to put all that information together and come up with something to explain why this firm is not operating productively. If my report causes a member of the staff embarrassment or shows him to be incompetent, then so be it. It certainly does not reflect on you. Now," he ended briskly, "if that's all, I'll get along and see Frank." Without waiting for her reply, he disappeared through the door.

Smothering her frustration and bewilderment, Julie turned her attention to her desk and the work piled on top. She sat down once more and after doggedly concentrating was able to make some progress, albeit less impressive than her usual standard.

Some time later she looked up to find Alex watching her. She threw down her pen and jumped to her feet, eyes wide and inquiring.

"What did he say?"

Alex smiled, coming toward her slowly, and Julie's heart turned over. He really was the most devastating man she had ever met.

"After the initial shock," Alex paused to light a cigarette, blowing the smoke sideways with a tilt of his head, "he congratulated me on my excellent taste."

Her face warm, Julie tried unsuccessfully to look unmoved. "You know what I mean, Alex," she pleaded. "Was he irritated that we hadn't acknowledged each other right at the beginning?"

"If he was he didn't say so."

"Is this going to make any difference to my job here?" she began anxiously.

"Of course not!" he exploded. "Don't be such an idiot. Why should it?"

She looked down at her desk, twisting her hands nervously. "I suppose I'm just concerned for my job because I've worked hard to get where I am and naturally I can't afford to jeopardize my future here."

"You are not dependent on this job, Julie, and you know it." Alex's lean features darkened with color, anger apparent in the twist of his mouth. "From the time you left, I deposited an allowance for you at the bank." His direct look held her own tawny one and she was helpless to look away. "You never used a dime of it. So, don't give me that garbage about needing this job to eat because I won't buy it." Savagely, he ground out the cigarette in the tray on top of her desk, his anger barely leashed as he strode toward the door of her office. "There is no point in discussing the past," he said bleakly. "For the next few months I think we should concentrate on making an honest effort to try to get along without any more rehashing of old grievances." He directed another of his unreadable looks at her set face. "Are you willing, Julie?"

Julie nodded numbly, grateful that his anger had cooled.

Alex acknowledged her acquiescence with a satisfied jerk of his dark head and turned to leave. Suddenly Julie recalled that he had not explained John Fisher's surprising attack.

"You were going to explain why John was so angry with me, Alex."

He considered her silently as he prepared to answer. "Let's just say that he is running scared right now and is pretty desperate to stop the inevitable from happening."

"What is inevitable?"

"The fact that he has been a less than loyal employee," Alex replied laconically.

"Why did he think I had anything to do with it?" Julie persisted, remembering the viciousness directed toward her and unable to suppress a shiver.

Instantly Alex's face softened. "Don't worry about it, Julie." His voice deepened as he comforted her. "He was mistaken and I will see to it that he's informed of that fact."

Still puzzled but accepting Alex's reassurance and perfectly willing to place her trust in his protection, Julie sank into her chair. After peering speculatively at her for a long moment, Alex backed out of the office, closing the door behind him.

* * *

Arriving at her apartment that evening, she immediately began sorting and boxing her things, her senses alert for Alex's arrival. She was not very far along when he appeared. After letting him in, she returned to packing a chest in the center of the room. Her glance lingered on his strong lithe legs in faded jeans with a knit pullover shirt of navy blue that darkened his gray eyes to midnight black. Her hands were busy but she was unable to prevent her eyes from returning repeatedly to his compelling figure. He was undeniably attractive to her and she was disconcerted to discover that he was returning her compulsive regard with a hungry look of his own. She had dressed for comfort in a gold velour jogging suit which allowed freedom of movement as she bent and reached to prepare her things to go. That it was subtly flattering to her tawny hair and eyes and that it hugged her softly rounded shape most provocatively did not go unnoticed by her husband.

Hastily she jumped up from the chest which bulged from its assorted contents.

"I'm not ready yet, Alex." Nervously she wiped her palms on her thighs, drawing Alex's eyes to the outline of her long legs in the clinging velour.

"No problem. We have all night," he replied suggestively, his eyes devouring her.

Desperately Julie grabbed an armful of sweaters which were neatly stacked nearby. If Alex kept looking at her like that, she knew she would be incapable of resisting him. In his arms his touch would ignite her already aroused desire for him and she knew she would go up like a bundle of straw. She thrust the sweaters into his hands. "You can start placing these into that case over there." She indicated one of a matched set of luggage safely on the far side of the room and hoped that out of close proximity to his magnetic appeal, that she would be able to retain some sort of control over her wayward body.

With a regretful sigh, Alex obediently crossed the room and began packing the case. "Looks like you have enough stuff here to outfit an army." He cast a comprehensive glance around the room with its boxes and cases, their contents spilling over untidily. "You won't need anything but your clothes and makeup . . . that sort of thing. There's no need for all the household items you must have collected."

"I'm only taking what's necessary," she replied shortly, disappearing into her bedroom. She pulled a chair over to the closet and climbed onto it to allow her to reach some shoes which were stored toward the back of the closet shelf. Stretching as far as she could, she was still unable to touch the shoes. Suddenly she felt the warm strength of Alex's hands clasp her waist firmly. Surprised, she gasped, losing her balance and fell off the chair landing hard against his chest. The suddenness of her fall caught him slightly off balance and they both fell onto the floor, Julie on top of Alex.

"See what you made me do!" she accused, looking into his face which wore a satisfied smile.

"I was trying to help," he insisted, "because you seemed to be having trouble climbing onto that shelf."

"I wasn't climbing onto the shelf," she denied hotly while noting the glinting humor in his eyes. At this distance she was assailed by memories of other times when she had gazed closely into those gray eyes and then they would darken with startling speed as Alex's emotions changed from a teasing banter to urgent desire. "You know I was just stretching to reach those shoes," she insisted breathlessly as the tenor of Alex's breathing deepened, his lids well down and concealing the expression in his eyes. With every ounce of awareness in her, Julie was conscious of the length of the hard body beneath her and she yearned with a feeling amounting almost to agony to yield the softness of her own femininity against that hardness.

Weakly she tried to push against his chest to move up and away from him, but Alex's hands enclosed her from behind, one hand firmly pressing her waist against his hard body while the other came up seductively underneath her hair and caressed her nape. For a few moments, they were completely absorbed in just watching each other, and Alex's eyes darkened passionately, his gaze wandering to her mouth and lingering there.

"No, Alex," she whispered, straining her face away from his.

"Yes," he replied huskily, his mouth coming closer to hers.

Julie wanted to resist him but was completely powerless under the spell of their mutual need for each other. A sweet languor invaded her senses. With a deep sigh, Alex suddenly turned over, carrying Julie with him. She felt the full weight of his body on hers and when his mouth claimed hers with a devastating urgency, her lips opened helplessly.

His kiss was a fierce possession of her senses and she gloried in the answering blaze of her response. His hands moved warmly and with familiar intimacy over her body, seeking those secret places only Alex knew would evoke a flaring need which only he could assuage.

"How I want you, Julie," he whispered hoarsely.

Through the clamoring of her senses, Julie heard Alex's involuntary words. She wanted him, too. She wanted to grab this moment and be damned with tomorrow. This was Alex, her love, her husband and he was inflamed with a desire for her to match her own. Tears spurted suddenly as the depth of her longing for Alex's love crept in to take the joy from her abandoned response to him. They trickled down her soft cheeks mingling with Alex's lips as he kissed her face.

With his awareness of her tears, he lifted his face and studied her intently, his breathing heavy and deep with the force of his unchecked passion.

"Julie?" He stared at her.

"Let me up, Alex." Her choked voice was muffled against his warm throat.

He was perfectly still as he registered her withdrawal. Then with a force of emotion barely contained, he rolled off her and onto his feet. Julie lay where she was, her tears still flowing and feeling a despair more defeating than anything she had ever known. She wanted Alex's love more than anything else in the world, and she wouldn't—she couldn't settle for anything less.

It was a wary and uncertain Julie who awoke the next morning. She opened the curtains to a beautiful, sunshiny day, its blatant beauty mocking the uneasy feeling in the pit of her stomach when she recalled the events of the previous evening. Heartened in spite of herself after peering out into the fresh brightness of the new day, Julie wondered about arrangements for breakfast.

She sighed deeply at the sight of boxes and luggage in various stages of being unpacked. She hated to leave them to Sarah but there was hardly any choice left to her. Perhaps Sarah would not mind too much, she thought hopefully, and from the months spent in this house earlier, she would recall that Julie had been a neat and thoughtful person, tidying her own room and taking as many household tasks upon herself as she was able to do within the confines of Mrs. Brandt's grudging approval. Resolutely determined not to dwell on the past, Julie dressed. A critical glance in the mirror revealed her coolly beautiful in a bright white skirt and peach silk blouse. She left her room and made her way quietly downstairs.

There was no one about as she entered the kitchen, but coffee had been made. She reached for a cup from the six hanging from a decorative holder near the pot and poured the hot fragrant brew. She gingerly sipped a few mouthfuls and set her cup down, carefully looking about for evidence that any breakfast had been planned by Alex or Mrs. Brandt. Nothing disturbed the neat, orderly kitchen and she decided to prepare something for Alex and herself since they would need to depart for the office at about the same time.

The contents of the refrigerator yielded eggs and bacon and she wrapped a towel around her waist and began to make a meal for her husband for the first time in almost two years. It gave her a keen and satisfying pleasure to be able to cook for Alex, and no amount of caution and stern lectures inside her head could prevent the happy feeling she got as she set the table for two and placed the food on the warmer ready for Alex when he came down. Even if she did not eat with him, the joy of knowing that she had prepared his breakfast brought a sweet satisfaction.

She was seated and buttering golden brown toast when she sensed his presence. She looked up quickly. He stood at the door, silently watching her, his eyes a dark slate-gray.

"What's all this?" His quizzical glance swept the table and the food ready on the warmer.

Julie's heart fluttered as she encouraged his familiar look. Alex always felt good early in the morning and his mood was usually teasing and loving to her when they first awakened. It would be easy to pretend that everything was the way it had been.

"Oh, good morning." Her breathless greeting was acknowledged by a slow smile as his gaze lingered on her glowing skin and the soft swell of her breasts under the shiny peach silk. "I had to make breakfast for myself and since it was no more trouble to make it for two I went ahead and made yours." Her tentative explanation drew no response other than his continued gaze at her flushed features. She moistened her lips uncertainly when he leaned away from the door jamb and walked toward her.

"This really is a treat," he said finally, coming to a stop just short of her and reaching for a cup. "I was down earlier and made some coffee but I never have breakfast anymore. I've gotten out of the habit." The last statement was delivered flatly.

Julie recalled the warm and loving breakfasts they had shared and the thought of Alex forgoing that meal was strangely disquieting. The feeling of regret that assailed her was only one more sad leftover of their former joy and happiness.

"I didn't hear you moving around this morning," she ventured shyly as he helped his plate from the counter. "You must have been up very early."

"I was." His back was to her so that Julie could not see whether his brief, noncommittal reply masked any other emotion.

"Are you always such an early riser?" Foolishly she probed, ignoring her own knowledge of this man whose habits and behavior she had learned early not to question.

He turned and directed a straight stare into her amber eyes.

"I usually wake up very early and when I do, I get up," he said evenly. "Once you think about it, I don't really have much reason for lying around in bed."

She flushed warmly, already regretting her strange urge to get at him.

He placed his plate across from her own and sat down, his large frame folding fluidly into the chair like a large black cat. A predatory cat, she thought involuntarily. She had probed and prodded like a foolish kitten and now she had a distinct feeling that he would retaliate.

"How about yourself," he drawled. "Do you languish in your bed in the mornings?"

"No, of course not," she choked, wishing desperately that she had never begun this ridiculous exercise. It was a foregone conclusion that in any verbal exchange Alex would demolish her and she gritted her teeth and tensed to prepare for the worst.

"My bed is just not what it used to be," Alex lamented. "Lonely and cold."

Julie looked longingly at the door wondering if she could get up and run out. Alex must have read her mind because his hand closed over her wrist and he continued conversationally.

"Does it bother you that my bed is lonely and cold, Julie?" he asked, his voice hardening as he stared into her golden eyes. "Just what did you have in mind when you started this little morning chat?" His thumb began a caressing movement over the delicate, sensitive skin of her wrist, evoking a thrill which was in no way diminished by the closeness of his face as he leaned near waiting for her reply.

"I didn't have anything in mind, Alex," she denied faintly, tugging to free her wrist. "I was just making conversation. You used to eat breakfast every morning and you used to love to lie in bed in the mornings. That's all I meant."

"I used to have a wife to keep me company, too, and every morning breakfast was a time to linger with her after we had made love . . . or had you forgotten?" he demanded savagely. He pushed her wrist from him, rising from the chair to turn his back to her. He thrust his hands through the black thickness of his hair, his back suggesting a restrained fury.

She winced at the savagery unleashed by her unthinking remarks. Her eyes filled with tears as she weakly rubbed her tender skin of her wrist. Clamping her lips rigidly, she refused to cry. After all, she had no one else to blame but her own foolish self, she thought bitterly.

Alex's voice penetrated the painful mist. "I didn't mean to yell at you, Julie. You shouldn't have tried to get at me like that."

Julie laughed shakily and lifted a napkin to wipe away the tears.

"I know," she said softly. "I don't know what made me want to antagonize you this morning, Alex. It certainly isn't a very good start at making a good impression on your mother." Her mouth twisted wryly. "At this rate her plan will fail even before it begins."

"Forget her plan!" Alex ground out.

His words echoed round the kitchen. Julie stared at his retreating back, the throbbing in her wrist forgotten in the surge of pain swamping her heart. The futile exercise enacted at the breakfast table was reminiscent of countless similar ones and bitter memories brought a taste of ashes to her suddenly dry mouth. Thanks to her stupid behavior, Alex had not even tasted the food she had prepared so lovingly. His shoulders sagged dejectedly. Only the sound of the door slamming violently penetrated the cold silence of the house.

Chapter Seven

Julie arrived at the office grimly determined to project a facade of cool composure for the benefit of the curious stares and speculation which she knew were directed at her and the sudden acknowledgement of her marriage to Alex. Anything less would invite questions from friends and acquaintances with whom she worked which she felt unable to parry. Of course, she thought wistfully, as Alex had indicated the day before, no one would dare question him, and she spared a moment to imagine herself handling awkward situations with the arrogant expertise which came naturally to her husband. The image of herself in command failed to stabilize in her mind, however, and with an inward shrug of resignation, she braced mentally for the ordeal.

Surprisingly, there was no problem. Candy greeted her with her usual warmth and the inevitable cup of coffee.

"Mr. Brandt came in earlier this morning, Julie, and asked me to tell you that his team intends to spend most of the morning in the conference room."

The sound of Alex's name caused a small tingle to course down her spine.

"Oh?" Her voice came out carefully normal.

Candy continued informatively. "He said to mention to you that the two of you would grab a quick lunch," she smiled teasingly, "but for you not to forget him and run off before he was free." Then with a meaningful look at Julie, "Though how you could forget lunch with a man like that is beyond me!"

"Thanks, Candy," Julie returned dryly.

Her secretary paused a moment uncertainly before rushing on. "I think this is the most romantic situation I've ever known. To be reunited with your husband . . . thrown into his company daily. It's fate, that's what it is," she sighed dreamily. "It's just wonderful!"

Shaking her head, Julie murmured something incoherent and escaped to the safety of her office, closing the door firmly before Candy followed and subjected her to more romantic imaginings on a situation that Julie was finding anything but romantic.

Alex had apparently already done some preparation before she arrived to explain their suddenly changed relationship, Julie reflected thoughtfully. She wondered about the message left with Candy regarding their arrangements for lunch. After the bitter scene at breakfast, it would be logical to assume that he would want to see very little more of his wife that day. But in his usual autocratic style she had been given her orders without any consultation and through a third person. She fumed vexedly.

With these unsettling thoughts, Julie resolutely put aside any further conjecture concerning her husband and attacked the morning mail. It came to her in some amusement a few minutes later that her work did not require quite the fierce attention it was receiving and relaxing somewhat, succeeded in turning out a reasonably profitable amount of work.

Surprisingly, the quick lunch with Alex that day began without any hostility from either of them. Determinedly, Julie kept her remarks to the business of the day and Alex, with a slightly sardonic air, seemed inclined to tolerate the wary truce. He discussed Peters-Winton with a perspicacity which both impressed and slightly overwhelmed his wife. Many of his comments concerning practices which were redundant and inefficient were indisputable and it occurred to Julie later when rethinking some of his remarks that they were really very basic and easily noted problem areas. Why it had taken an expert to single them out was surprising, all things considered. Of course, just that kind of expertise was what Alex was being paid for and Julie reluctantly acknowledged that she glowed with pride that he excelled at his work. She was thrilled, too, that he freely discussed his work with her. However, after some consideration she concluded rather contrarily that he used her more or less as a sounding board for his thoughts. She realized ruefully that he didn't expect her to agree or disagree. With somewhat mixed feelings at this thought, she grew quiet and withdrawn midway through the meal.

"Have I lost my audience?" Alex's amused voice penetrated her abstraction.

"What makes you think that?" She watched him warily through her lashes.

His mouth compressed impatiently. "Come on, Julie. We were talking companionably one moment and next thing I know we were no longer communicating." He made a sharp motion with his hand. "You weren't even in the same world with me."

"I didn't think you noticed," she retorted grimly.

"What is that supposed to mean?"

She clicked her tongue impatiently. "It's the same old thing, Alex. You weren't discussing anything with me. You were just thinking out loud and I happened to be at the same table with you."

He directed an uncompromising stare into her eyes. "So you think anyone would have done just as well, that I'm talking to you only because you happen to be here. Do I have that right?"

"Yes!" she answered defiantly. "You issued my orders for lunch through Candy this morning and now here we are."

What was the matter with her? she thought, anguished. One moment she was glowing with pride over Alex and the next she was attacking him like a shrew. It was going to be a miracle if he could stand the sight of her after a few more days of her erratic moods.

"If you didn't want to have lunch with me, you could have refused," he pointed out calmly, his look intent, assessing her flushed features almost clinically.

"How could I refuse," she cried, "when Candy and everybody else in the entire building is watching us with bated breath to see what's going to happen next in this . . ." her voice wobbled tremulously, "this charade!"

Alex's gaze never wavered. Under his penetrating regard, Julie averted her face. Her throat tightened with the effort not to burst into tears. Desperately, she delved into her purse searching for a tissue as her eyes filled and overflowed. Gratefully, she grabbed the snow white handkerchief silently proffered by her unperturbable husband.

As discreetly as possible she mopped her eyes, taking huge deep gulps of air in an agony of embarrassment, horrified at her emotional display in a public place. Alex would be certain to wish to see the back of her forever, she thought miserably. She chanced a quick look at him from beneath her lashes, spiked by tears and slightly smudged from their recent drenching.

Unable to interpret his silence and squirming with embarrassment over her display of immaturity, which she was sure Alex was thinking, Julie longed to escape.

"What was that all about?" Alex inquired with weary patience. "I get the distinct feeling that the real issue here has not been mentioned yet."

Looking up into his face suddenly, she was surprised to find a look of tenderness in Alex's eyes. To her consternation, her eyes filled with tears again. If he chose to treat her gently right now, she would lose complete control.

He smiled slowly into her eyes. "I don't suppose you would consider telling me the real reason why you're upset, would you?" She mopped her eyes yet again and looked around cautiously hoping to seize an opportune moment to escape the restaurant to a more private place to try and gain some control over her wayward emotions.

As though divining her thoughts, Alex pushed back his chair and stood close at her side while she gathered her purse and turned to leave. At the door, he paid the check quickly, one hand detaining her by the arm and preventing any escape from the battery of eyes she felt sure were staring at her.

That he was perfectly aware of her embarrassment was proven when he remarked calmly, "Relax, no one noticed your distress, Julie. They were all too busy enjoying lunch. I just wish you had enjoyed yours." His voice was lightly teasing as he looked down at the tawny head which barely reached the top of his shoulder. "Let's walk there to that park bench." And without waiting for her consent, he guided her down the steps and across the street where a small public area contained benches placed among flowering shrubs, brilliant in spring sunshine and blossom.

His calm acceptance of her bizarre behavior in a public place soothed her heated nerves and Julie subsided onto the bench with him, grateful for the relative privacy of the gardens and for a few moments to gather her shattered composure.

Turning slightly toward her, Alex lifted his arm and placed it along the back of the bench. With his other hand, he tipped her chin up gently, forcing her to look directly into his gray eyes, eyes that she noted were at this moment dark and compelling, seriously intent as he sought to read the message of her own.

His mouth quirked in gentle amusement. "You are beautiful even when you cry, do you know that?"

She flushed and attempted to turn her head away, feeling the magnetism of his attraction for her and anxious lest he sense how completely he could overpower her senses in her shaken state. He refused to release her chin, however, and she dropped her eyes before the frankly sensual look in his own. She was weakly determined not to succumb to any persuasion he might choose to employ and made a valiant effort to gather her thoughts.

"I'm sorry I cried in there," she began huskily. Clearing her throat, she began again. "I don't know what's the matter with me, Alex. I don't intend to start these ridiculous scenes . . ."

"Do you mean like that one this morning?" he asked patiently.

She winced. "Well, yes. Before I realized it, we were fighting again and I don't think I can stand much more." She looked into his face. "I don't think this is going to work."

"Yes, it is going to work," he asserted firmly. "You're making this more difficult than it needs to be, honey." Julie's heart lurched at the casual endearment. "Stop fighting and analyzing everything." He laughed quietly as he leaned down and kissed the tip of her nose. "Relax and trust me for a little while and let's see how that works, hm?" His hand released her chin and slid down her throat, where his thumb caressed the pulse that fluttered there in response to his touch. Her lashes came down to hide from his sharp sight the eager response which flared in her eyes, golden and bright from recent tears.

"Are you willing, Julie?" His fingers tightened briefly, compelling her compliance.

She sighed, "I'll try."

Julie was drawn out of her musings by Alex's next words.

"Were your worst fears realized when your colleagues learned you were a married woman?" His quizzical look captured her startled one.

"What do you mean?" Flustered, she dropped her gaze.

"Your little secretary didn't demand an explanation?"

"Of course not! Don't be ridiculous."

His shoulders shook with silent laughter. "What!

Don't tell me your changed marital status didn't provoke lots of delicious gossip," he tormented.

With a painful assumption of dignity, Julie replied, "You may find this entire situation amusing, Alex, but just remember that I have to remain in my job after you have finished here and left. I just want to salvage some sort of decent reputation after you've gone."

His smiled faded slightly and he favored her with a tender look. "Don't worry, baby, I'll personally see to it that you are well taken care of after I'm gone."

Her heart lurched painfully. She didn't want to think about the time when Alex would once again be out of her life. The fact that he could laugh about it hurt unbearably and she felt an irresistible urge to retaliate.

"You're right, Alex," she said brightly. "There were lots of opportunities for me to better myself in the past year that I didn't capitalize on. Now that my skeletons are out of the closet, I probably will be taking advantage of those opportunities."

His smile hardened and his eyes took on a silvery hue.

"Careful, little cat. Don't threaten me or you might find that you have undertaken more than you can handle."

So much for wounding him. His hide was as thick as the jungle animal he resembled as he uncoiled smoothly from the bench, pulling her up with him.

His hard glance surveyed her crestfallen face and he laughed suddenly, his good humor restored. He hugged her hard, pressing her tightly against his warm chest. Unaccountably comforted, she walked alongside him as they headed back to the office.

Things settled into a more or less uneventful routine after that. Working together was satisfying and fulfilling to Julie and she felt that Alex enjoyed the undeniable rapport between them during the day. Once at home, they generally had a drink together and, with Sarah's help, Julie assisted in preparing dinner. Alex's mother joined them sometimes for dinner but at others she stayed in her own room, eating from a tray. Suspecting that Mrs. Brandt wished to throw them together to enjoy their dinner alone as often as possible, Julie cooperated even though she knew it made little difference to Alex whether they ate intimately alone or with his mother. Still, she willingly played along with whatever her mother-in-law or Alex suggested. After all, she thought ruefully, that was the reason she was here.

Apparently, the front presented by Julie and Alex to Mrs. Brandt was fairly convincing; her expression as she watched them lit up hopefully when she thought herself unobserved. Her attitude toward Julie in the time since she had returned had been thoughtful and anxious. Not certain that her daughter-in-law was completely comfortable in the same house with her, Mrs. Brandt made hesitant overtures to Julie which in the past would have been unheard of. Julie, her nature naturally generous and forgiving, accepted the change in her mother-in-law with a mixed sense of regret and chagrin. It was impossible not to think regretfully of the time when acceptance of Alex's wife would have made the first months of their marriage easier, and now that the way was smoothed for her acceptance, Julie was forced to play the charade conceived by her husband for love of his mother and not his wife. The irony of it was almost amusing if it was not so painful.

Some nights Alex disappeared into his den, that special hideaway which she felt reluctant to enter under the conditions of their present relationship. Usually he would murmur something about having papers that needed his attention and, slightly wary and cool, would take leave of his mother and more often than not brusquely wish Julie a good night. On those occasions she usually did not see him until the next morning when they had breakfast.

Julie was happiest during breakfast. With the sun streaming through the polished glass of the breakfast room and sitting across from her husband, she could almost feel that hers was a normal marriage and they were a normal couple sharing the special time of morning when spirits are revived and hopeful and life good. And so, time passed swiftly until Julie had been living at home again for several weeks.

At the office, most of the background information required to complete Alex's report on Peters-Winton had been compiled and he spent less time there. Mr. Peters was eagerly awaiting the report from Alex which would recommend any changes considered necessary to revitalize the organization. Without his presence to constantly remind her of the irresistible appeal he still held for her, Julie managed to establish some semblance of order in her life, while still at another level she longed passionately for some indication from Alex that the status quo was as unsatisfying to him as it was to her.

Unfortunately, no such indication was forthcoming from her inscrutable husband. His intentions remained as obscure to Julie as ever. He patiently indulged his mother while successfully shrugging aside Julie's protests when she complained of the dishonesty of their actions.

"Just leave it, Julie," he advised offhandedly when she chafed at another deception one night done solely for the benefit of his mother.

"But I feel so awful about the dishonesty of the whole thing," she explained earnestly.

There was no reply as Alex carefully fitted together two fragile sections of wood on the minute bow of a model ship he was building.

"Hand me that glue, will you?" he muttered, the lines on his brow creased in concentration.

Exasperated, she lifted the tube and passed it to him. She waited until he could let go of one piece to hold the tube, directing the point exactly, showing the kind of attention to detail, even in a hobby done for pleasure, which he exhibited in his professional life.

With the tiny procedure completed, he looked up encountering the exasperation in her golden eyes. Immediately, his own eyes crinkled with humor.

"Feeling a little neglected?" he teased.

She tossed her head angrily, instantly responding to his taunt, her anxious concern of a few moments before forgotten.

"What do you mean, neglected?"

He slanted a wicked look at her face, wrinkled in puzzlement. "I mean, my little honey, that you're getting grouchy and grumpy," ignoring her indrawn gasp of indignation, "so I naturally assumed you were bored, feeling neglected, you know what I mean," he finished blandly.

"I'm not bored! That's not what I was getting at

and you know it!" she declared hotly. "I just wanted to let you know that I feel awful about this deception we are carrying on for the benefit of your mother." Agitatedly, she directed an imploring look at her husband, whose expression was anything but sympathetic. Instead, the look on his face suggested his thoughts were not even remotely concerned with the subject at hand.

"Carrying on, you say," he repeated lazily, laughing as her cheeks flamed at the look in his eyes. "Any carrying on I might do would certainly not be for the benefit of my mother, but for my own benefit." Leaning toward her slightly, he captured her wrist and pulled her toward him.

Caught off guard, she tumbled against his chest.

"Alex, let me up," she objected breathlessly. Any contact with his lean, masculine form caused her heartbeat to accelerate. The tiny pulse in her throat throbbed furiously, and raising her eyes to his, Julie saw that Alex was watching the telltale quiver. At the expression in his dark eyes, all resistance weakened and she gazed helplessly at his face, sensual and closed as his eyes continued to roam over her features, his gaze almost physical in its intensity. Her breathing quickened and she desperately pushed against his chest, needing distance to free herself from his overwhelming attraction.

His arms tightened fractionally and any escape was prevented as he lowered his head.

"Hm, you smell good," he breathed huskily, his mouth near her ear.

Julie felt his hand caressing her throat, sensually stroking the sensitive skin while his other hand gently rubbed her back and shoulders, randomly searching and distributing warmth which spread throughout her body. Weakly Julie tried to resist the almost irresistible pleasure which Alex offered.

Unhurriedly he explored her face, his lips brushing lightly across her eyes and cheeks, moving around to nuzzle under her chin. All the while he avoided her mouth and soon she forgot all effort to resist as he skillfully coaxed her complete arousal. It became imperative that she have the completeness of his kiss, but still Alex denied her.

Sighing impotently, Julie's hands came up alongside his face, lovingly nestling into the familiar planes, guiding his mouth toward her own. She knew he was deliberately prolonging his caresses, but she no longer cared. It was only important that he should never stop.

"Alex." Her unconscious plea went unheeded.

Tantalizingly, he kissed each corner of her mouth, lightly and teasingly. A tension was building inside her, leading inexorably toward a joy and pleasure she had been too long denied.

"Kiss me properly, Alex," she urged, returning his kisses a little desperately while he denied her his mouth. Alex's hands had somehow lowered the zipper on her lounging robe and it slipped easily down to her waist. His black head descended to one creamy breast, his thumb sensually moving back and forth coaxing to a hardened peak the swelling fullness. When his mouth touched the throbbing globe, she gasped with the pleasure streaking through her senses. Her head dropped back baring her throat welcoming the intimate exploration he was conducting so carefully. Totally abandoned were any thoughts of resistance. No longer did she wish to withhold from Alex any part of herself. So completely were her defenses shattered that she was unaware of time or place or space. Only Alex and the pleasure he evoked was real.

"Touch me, Julie," he commanded.

Already her hands were stroking his chest, running down his lean length and up around his shoulders, delving into the muscle and bone of his warm body. Quickly, he shed his shirt, tugging it over his head, thrusting it aside. The heat of his skin and the masculine scent of him filled her senses. Eagerly she allowed him to push her down upon the couch and when his hard length pressed against her, she moaned with anticipation of his complete possession.

"Darling Julie," Alex whispered, his mouth moving sensually against her throat and down over the peaks and valleys of her breasts. Frantically Julie sought his lips and when Alex finally covered her mouth with his own, she shuddered, her lips opening to accept ecstatically the plundering of her senses which his careful seduction had ensured. Over and over again she strained to accept his kisses, oblivious of everything except the need to assuage the terrible tension clamoring for that ultimate fulfillment.

When Alex stood suddenly and lifted her into his arms, there was no thought of denial.

"Don't fight me, darling." Urgently, he buried his face in her hair, inhaling the fragrance of it, then looking deeply into her eyes he willed her consent. The languor induced by their hunger for each other still pervaded her mind and limbs and Julie was incapable of denying him. So aroused was she that the jangling of the telephone across the room barely pierced her clouded mind.

Alex smothered a curse, looking at the offending

instrument, indecision holding him immobile with Julie still in his arms.

"Oh, God, no, not now."

Insistently the phone continued to ring. Reluctantly setting her down, he reached for the telephone, savagely wrenching it from the cradle.

"Alex Brandt here."

Turning her back, Julie fumblingly pulled her gown up, slipping her arms through the sleeves and reaching awkwardly behind her to pull up the zipper. She groped unsuccessfully for a moment, then felt Alex's hands, warm and steady, slowly pull the zipper up and secure it with a gentle pat. Quickly, she stepped aside, her legs trembling weakly in the aftermath of the storm of desire, torn between frustration and relief. Without that phone call, Julie knew she surely would have allowed Alex to take her to his bed where he would have possessed her completely. And she had offered no resistance.

Suddenly she became aware of a tenseness in Alex as he listened to the caller on the other end of the line. Warily, he glanced over at Julie as the voice from the receiver in his hand carried clearly to strike an agonizing blow to her fragile defenses. It was Angela, her saccharine voice raised playfully while she awaited Alex's reply.

"I really can't talk right now, Angela," he said tersely while Angela could be heard determinedly coaxing.

With an impatient frown, whether in irritation or concern, Julie was unsure, Alex brusquely terminated the conversation, promising a return call from his office the next day.

A deadly silence settled when he replaced the

receiver. Alex ran his hands tiredly through his hair as he cast an assessing look at Julie, who remained stonily silent.

"That has got to be the worst timed telephone call of my entire life," he said wryly.

"I think I'll go to bed," Julie choked, turning for the door.

Alex reached out a long arm, grasping her as she would have turned the corner.

"Please give me a chance to explain, Julie."

"You don't have to explain anything to me, Alex." Tiredly, Julie looked into his face. Not five minutes ago she had been kissing every inch of that face. Rage and frustration rose bitterly in her throat. She braced to resist the urge to bring her hand up and rake her nails against his hard cheek. In despair, she closed her eyes, unwanted tears flooding them.

"Please, darling," Alex began, the gray of his eyes dark as wet slate, his grip on her arm painful in its intensity. "You've got to let me explain."

"Take your hands off me this minute."

Lifting her chin, Julie directed a gold stare into Alex's pale features. As he met the unmistakable glitter in her eyes, Alex's mouth tightened angrily.

"I don't want you to leave me before we talk about this. You can't walk out now."

"Want to bet?" Yanking her arm out of his grasp, Julie ran.

Chapter Eight

Safely in her own room, Julie dashed scalding tears from her cheeks. She would not give him the satisfaction of knowing that she could still be wounded by anything Angela did. The truth that Julie had been refusing to acknowledge rose inexorably in her mind. She had never stopped loving Alex. In fact, her love had strengthened since their separation. Absence from him and refusing to think of him had not killed the overwhelming depth of her love for her husband. Bitterly she acknowledged that he had only to touch her, even come into the same room with her, for that love to invade her entire being. He made her feel alive again. And to be alive meant to suffer the pain and torture of being denied his love in return. Tears welled in her eyes again and slowly trickled down the softly rounded curve of her cheek.

She secured the lock on her door. Alex must not learn how terribly vulnerable she had become in the few short weeks she had been exposed to him again.

She tensed as she heard him outside the door.

"Julie." Quietly he spoke her name. "Open the door."

Julie remained rooted in the center of the room

131

staring at the closed door, her chest rising and falling with each agitated breath.

"I said open this door," Alex growled, still not raising his voice but ordering her compliance by the very intensity of his tonc.

Knowing that he would force the door if she did not comply, she whirled around and rushed into the bathroom where she turned on the shower. The sound of the spray would carry outside her room and she knew Alex would think she was bathing. As a matter of fact, she thought grimly, I might as well just do that. She quickly unzipped the robe which fell in a soft swish to the floor. She stepped out of her panties and kicked them aside, heedless of her usual neat habits. She then closed and locked the bathroom door.

The shower spray was too cold when she stepped under it and she gasped a little, but in her agitation the temperature of the water was hardly noticed. For timeless moments, she stood under the stinging spray not thinking anything, simply allowing the water to cascade over her body, onto her scalp, wetting her hair and running into her face. In spite of her determination not to give in to the temptation to cry, she began to whimper like an animal in pain. Soon she was weeping unrestrainedly, tears coursing and mixing with the water as she gave herself up to the hopelessness of her love.

Julie did not know how long she wept or how long she continued to stand drooping with pain, but after a while she reached out mechanically and turned off the water. She groped for a towel, rubbed it lethargically over her hair and skin, then carelessly dropped it on the floor. She unlocked the bathroom door and walked into her room heading directly for the bed.

She did not bother to put on a nightgown, but pulled back the covers of her bed, crawled into it, exhaustion and unhappiness dulling her senses. She pulled the covers up under her chin, curling herself into a tight ball. Like a black cloud, sleep swept over her instantly.

The next morning Julie awoke and lay quietly as she groped to understand the heavy feeling in her chest. The events of the night before were not long in returning to her consciousness. She winced with the pain of loss as Angela's return into Alex's life must surely represent the end of any hopes Julie might have cherished for a new beginning in her marriage.

It was late already, she noted as she turned her head on the pillow and looked disinterestedly at the face of the clock. Hopefully Alex was up and out of the house. Sometime today she would sort out what to say to him when she returned from work. It was impossible to stay in the house when any moment her feelings for Alex could overwhelm her. There was no point in lying to herself; Alex had only to touch her and she was his. She must not let that happen when he was not prepared to make any permanent commitment.

She got out of bed and washed and dressed quickly. Looking at herself critically in the long mirror framed and standing free in the corner of her room, she felt satisfied that the facade she presented projected the image she needed. She was chic in a black linen blazer over a tan dress. Her signature scarf of black and tan perfectly complemented the outfit and her hair was honey smooth, tucked under, cupping beneath her chin. She was totally unaware of the delicate and vulnerable look of her tremulous mouth and chin as she lifted her head proudly. She reached for a black kid shoulder bag and unlocked her door.

No one was stirring, she thankfully noted, and skipping breakfast, she totally avoided the kitchen area of the house. Quietly, she let herself out of the house and got into her car. Alex, she thought, must still be at home as his car was in its usual spot alongside hers.

Since she arrived at Peters-Winton late, the morning was hectic and she gratefully threw herself into the fray. Anything to keep from dwelling on how to tell Alex that she did not intend to keep up the pretense of their marriage. Time and again during the day, she sternly admonished herself when without warning she would think longingly of Alex, of how much she loved him, and her futile hope that this time their marriage would succeed. Refusing to succumb to the treachery of her weakness for him was the only way to get out of the situation with her pride intact. Ironically, she acknowledged that it was too late to salvage her heart.

A few minutes before lunch, the buzzer sounded on the intercom system on her desk. Pushing the button, Julie answered.

"Mr. Peters wants to see you in his office, Julie," Candy's voice informed her through the transmitter.

"Thanks, Candy. Any special time?"

"Just when it's convenient, Doris said." Doris was Frank Peters' secretary and as Julie arrived at his office, she was greeted warmly by the petite, graying woman.

"You can go right in, Julie," she smiled, looking up from her typewriter. "He has been expecting you."

"Oh, I hope I haven't kept him waiting. I was only just informed that he wanted to see me."

"Don't worry. Your husband is in there and Mr. Peters enjoys talking to him anytime." She turned back to her typewriter and dismissed Julie vaguely as she frowned over the notebook containing her notes.

Julie paled at the mention of Alex. She had not been aware that he was at Peters-Winton today. Usually he looked in at her office when he was in the building. But after last night, she thought miserably, it was just as well that he had chosen to avoid her. It saved me the trouble, she thought darkly. Her hand went to her throat and she quickly lowered it to knock on the closed door.

"Come in," came the pleasant tones of her employer.

Taking a deep breath, Julie pushed open the door and entered. Immediately her eyes sought those of her husband, who lounged negligently on the black leather armchair which was placed so that its occupant could see both who entered the office and Frank Peters, seated behind the desk. Trust Alex to catch her unprepared, she thought waspishly as she averted her head, ignoring him and smiling warmly at Frank Peters.

"Candy says you wanted to see me, Mr. Peters."

"Sit down, Julie." He gestured to the chair placed close to the one which Alex occupied. "Alex and I were just discussing the results of his study for the company." He smiled archly. "Of course, you probably know what he has found. Probably talked it over at the breakfast table, eh?" He grinned fondly at his favorite employee.

As she eased gingerly into the chair, Julie glanced

briefly at her husband, whose shuttered face revealed nothing.

"I don't think I know what you're getting at, Mr. Peters," she said, pointedly ignoring Alex. "What is it that Alex has found?"

She concentrated her gaze on Mr. Peters' benign features. Whatever Alex hoped to prove by sitting with a blank look on his face escaped her, but she was equally determined not to give him the satisfaction of knowing he irritated her.

"Well, of course, I'm talking about the results of the management survey I commissioned him to perform." Peters tapped a report lying on his desk bound and lettered in black and gold. Peering forward, Julie could see the name of Alex's firm.

"Alex tells me that you have been extremely helpful to him and his staff as they collected all the information necessary to do this study, Julie, and I thought it would be interesting to you as someone who has contributed directly," again he bestowed another proud smile at her, "to hear the results right away before I call a general staff meeting."

Julie smiled stiffly. "Naturally I'm interested in hearing the results of the study." Quietly, she rearranged her skirt, crossing her slim ankles delicately and turned expectantly toward Alex. Looking at a point about an inch above his head, she hoped she looked suitably interested and composed as she prepared to bear the next few minutes in Alex's company.

"We make it a point not to discuss business at breakfast, don't we, Julie?" Silkily, he leveled his voice at her.

Her tawny eyes sparkled as they encountered the stormy gray of his. Startled, Julie realized Alex was furiously angry. In confusion, she dropped her eyes, her hands twisted tightly in her lap. Why was he so angry, she wondered bewilderedly. Surely it was she who had every right to be angry.

She looked up into the lean, dark planes of his face. Her eyes picked out the harsh lines etched alongside his mouth, usually sensually full and generous, but now stretched thin. A closer look at his body showed that he was not lounged casually in the chair, but tension emanated from his coiled length. He seemed poised for instant action.

"No, we don't discuss business at breakfast," she agreed quietly.

Mr. Peters nodded understandingly. "I guess I can see why you wouldn't," and winked at Alex meaningfully. "Anyway, Julie, your department figured heavily in the report and I'm proud to tell you that Alex commended the manner in which you run it and the way in which you supervise your little group."

"Why, thank you, Mr. Peters." Julie felt her face flush with pleasure and the quick look she flashed at Alex collided with the silvery gray of his stare. He would never make such a statement if it were not entirely deserving, she knew, and because of that, the compliment was even more valuable. Still, her pleasure faded in the cold glare of his eyes.

Mr. Peters, unaware of any hidden currents, continued more soberly. "Others have not been so efficient as you, I'm sorry to say. We have discovered that one member of my staff is guilty of collusion, among other things. Thanks to Alex here, we have learned that even before submitting our bids on certain jobs, our secrets were sold to our competitors." He threw a bleak look at Julie. "At least I know now why so much of the new business contracts I sought kept eluding me." He laughed uncomfortably. "I thought I was losing my touch and was seriously considering unloading the business and taking an early retirement." He brightened and grinned cheerfully. "I've decided I'm not ready to be put out to pasture after all."

"Contracts and bid packages," Julie repeated. She looked quickly at Alex. "John Fisher," she breathed wonderingly.

"Yes, John Fisher." He met her glance coolly. "Does that explain why he confronted you that morning?"

"Of course. No wonder he was so upset. He must have known then that you were close to discovering what he was up to." Forgetting her intention to remain coolly aloof, she flashed a warm smile at her husband.

He shifted his weight in the chair, his gray eyes enigmatic as he met the warmth in her smile.

Julie's smile faltered. She sensed the barely leashed fury held rigidly in check and longed to escape the confines of the small room. Without understanding it, she knew that Alex was biding his time to get her alone, and desperately she wished she was elsewhere.

Alex rose suddenly to his feet, causing an involuntary start in Julie. He smiled coldly down at her and reached for her wrist.

"We're going back to Julie's office for a moment, Frank," he explained, his voice casual. Only Julie was aware of the latent violence emanating from him as his fingers closed tightly around the delicate bones of her wrist. He pulled her to her feet.

"Right, right," Peters agreed jovially. "The staff meeting is scheduled for two o'clock this afternoon, Alex. They've all been notified. See you then."

Alex didn't turn around but continued holding Julie's gaze with his own. Stiffly, she allowed herself to be pushed out the door ahead of him.

When the door closed behind them, she turned angrily to Alex, tugging ineffectively at her imprisoned wrist.

"Turn me loose, Alex."

"When we get to your office." Grimly he strode ahead pulling her with him.

"What is the matter with you?" she demanded between clenched teeth, looking wildly around hoping Alex's high-handed behavior would go unnoticed until they were safely in her own office.

Candy looked up at their arrival, eyes widening at the set look of Alex's features and Julie's mutinous mouth. She watched speechlessly as they passed her desk and entered Julie's office.

Once behind the closed door, Alex released her wrist, keeping his body between the door and Julie as if anticipating a desire on her part to escape.

"Why did you leave the house this morning without seeing me first?" he demanded, his angry gaze fastened on her face.

She turned her back to him and moved over to the wide window which overlooked the city.

"I didn't want to see you this morning."

"Didn't you think there was some unfinished business between us?" Julie felt the conscious effort he made to maintain an even tone.

Her shoulders squared imperceptibly as she considered his question.

"Perhaps there was, but I can't imagine that you were too terribly upset." She paused before adding sarcastically, "Didn't Angela console you?"

"Julie, I didn't expect Angela to call last night."

"I'll bet you didn't."

She felt the surge of anger sweep through him as he grabbed her arm and jerked her around.

"Look at me!" His eyes fairly blazed, their silvery color flashing. He shook her briefly but violently. "We are going to have this out once and for all," he threatened, unheeding of the strength in his hands gripping her shoulders.

"You can't tell me what to do anymore, Alex," she said defiantly, "even if you shake my head off. I don't have to talk to you if I don't want to," she paused for effect, "and I don't want to."

Her words penetrated the haze of anger clouding Alex's mind. A mixture of expressions crossed his face. In the grip of fierce anger he had hurt her unconsciously. Fleetingly, he glanced down at his hands still clutching her shoulders and dropped them instantly. His eyes traveled over her ashen face and disheveled hair. He rubbed one hand over his face and she saw with shock that he was trembling.

"I didn't intend to approach you like this," he muttered. "I just knew it was vital that we talk about last night and when you left without a word this morning I was frantic to see you."

Julie watched Alex warily. Not many times had she seen him out of control and she tried to concentrate on what he was saying while one part of her brain reeled from the shock of the violent treatment he had subjected her to.

Trembling with reaction, she moved to her chair and sank weakly into it. She leaned her head over and rested it against her hands propped on her elbows.

"You're incredibly angry, Alex," she whispered tiredly. "I don't think this is a good time for us to talk."

"We can't leave it like this, Julie." He would have come around behind her desk, but when Julie stiffened involuntarily on recognizing his intention, he subsided into the chair. "I know you don't plan to return home tonight, do you?"

She raised her chin aggressively. "Can you blame me?"

He raked his fingers wearily through the jet thickness of his hair.

"Look, the staff meeting is scheduled for early afternoon. I think I can wrap it up in a couple of hours." He inhaled deeply. "Frank is depending on me to present the suggestions for improvement to his staff in such a way that they will want to cooperate. It's vital that they accept any changes willingly." He raised his eyes to meet hers in a direct look. "As soon as I conclude the meeting I want you to leave with me. Will you?"

Julie dropped her eyes to focus on the familiar objects on her desk. With everything in her she wanted to go with Alex. She wanted him to explain to her satisfaction why Angela called, wanted to be persuaded that continuing as they were was still possible and not a ridiculous dream.

With difficulty she raised her eyes to Alex's compelling gaze and nodded.

She registered the quick flash of relief on his face. Naturally he was pleased that he had once again pressured her into complying with his wishes, but for a moment she had glimpsed a depth of feeling which surprised her in Alex. It was almost as if in ensuring that she agreed to go with him, he had surmounted an important hurdle. Quickly dismissing her thoughts as wishful thinking, she began to purposefully shuffle the papers which were scattered over the surface of her desk.

"I need to get some work done, Alex," she said dismissingly in an effort to dispel the atmosphere which lingered from the heat of their argument. She longed to lose herself in the routine of her work, to hold at bay the worry and pain of dwelling on the state of her relationship with Alex.

The smile which he directed at her was faintly sardonic. With a slight nod of his head and an unmistakable look of triumph in his gray eyes, he left her office.

The drive home was accomplished with Alex's big car following close behind her. The rest of the day Alex had not sought her out, seeming satisfied to wait until he could give his undivided attention to their problem. Julie, too, was content to use the time to compose herself for what promised to be at best an interesting talk with Alex once they were home.

Soon they were entering the trimmed and clipped driveway. Nervously Julie collected her purse and placed her hand on the door handle. Alex suddenly appeared by her car, preventing her from pushing open the door.

"How would you like to have dinner out tonight, Julie?" Quietly, his voice deep and compelling, Alex awaited her reply.

"If that's what you want, Alex, then I have no objection." Actually, what they had to say to each other might prove easier to bear in the impersonal atmosphere of a public place, Julie thought bleakly.

If her unfeeling reply affected him, Alex refused to reveal his reaction. Nodding his head in satisfaction, he allowed her to push the door open and get out of the car. Together they walked to the entrance.

"Put on something special. Although you always look beautiful, this place we're going to is unique and I think you will enjoy it."

Her breath caught in her throat at the sound of his voice and the casual comment on her beauty. It sounded sincere and once more Julie puzzled at her failure to understand him. Why would he treat her at times as though she were really something special, as if he sincerely thought she was beautiful and desirable, while still maintaining contact with Angela, whose blatant designs on him could not be mistaken? Did Alex expect her to tolerate his double life? Even if it meant she could never see him again, their marriage never be complete, she knew she could not accept Alex on those terms.

"I thought we would head up the north shore to a little restaurant that I stumbled on a few months ago," he said offhandedly, cupping her elbow warmly in his hand. "They make a great lobster."

Her treacherous memory leaped back in time to the occasions when she and Alex had combed the Atlantic coastline looking for special places which featured Julie's favorite food.

She threw him a quick, searching look.

"Haven't lost your taste for lobster, have you?" he teased, his eyes roving over her face, lingering briefly on her tremulous mouth before traveling up to her eyes, tawny and veiled with their thick fringe of lashes.

Shaking her head wordlessly, she swallowed around the suddenly tight constriction in her throat, turning away from the message glinting in Alex's eyes.

"Alex, I . . ."

Ignoring her attempt to speak, he continued. "We'll have a quick drink and say hello to Mother. After you're dressed, we'll be off." His arm stretched out to open the ornate front door and lightly brushed against her breasts.

Her sharply indrawn breath at the unexpected contact was clearly audible, but Alex gave no indication that he noticed. Flushing, she strove to maintain an unruffled expression and they entered the house.

The sound of voices could be heard drifting from the living room, and frowning, Alex placed his hand on her waist, ushering her along toward the sound without inquiring whether or not she wished to go with him.

There was no chance of resisting his determined hand compelling her forward and as soon as her gaze focused on the scene in the elegant room, all thought of doing so fled. Her mother-in-law and Angela Roswell were seated and at first glance seemed to be enjoying a late afternoon visit. Barely touched cups of tea revealed that Angela's visit had barely begun. Dainty cakes and sandwiches were arranged on a small table in front of them.

Julie was vaguely aware of her mother-in-law's look, an odd mixture of wariness and appeal. However, to Julie's fragile composure, already strained in anticipation of what was soon to come with Alex, Angela's presence was shattering indeed.

"Just in time, darling," Angela's bright greeting was intended only for Alex. "Your mother and I have hardly begun to enjoy a little visit. Have a drink with us." Her mouth curved into an intimate smile showing flawless teeth and reminding Julie of a sleek cat who is about to get the cream.

"I know your habits well enough not to offer you tea at this hour." The hard crystal blue of her eyes, contrasting strikingly with her black hair, met Julie's. With something like a jolt, Julie felt the impact.

Alex's hand at Julie's waist tightened momentarily and he stiffened slightly. Nothing was revealed in his face as Julie's eyes flew involuntarily to his and then quickly away.

"I didn't expect to see you here, Angela," he said, his sardonic greeting civil but hardly warm with welcome. "How was Mexico City?"

In confusion, Julie tried to make sense of what was going on. Hadn't Alex seen Angela that afternoon? During their conversation the previous night he had suggested that she call him. Had she been in Mexico City and not here in Boston?

Angela's hard laugh was forced as she determinedly continued. "I've been back for a few days. I couldn't wait to see you and Margaret." She spared a quick look at his mother before turning her possessive gaze back to Alex. "Did you miss me?"

Ignoring the provocative question, Alex removed his hand from Julie's waist, sliding it down to enclose her wrist in his strong fingers. He pulled her along with him as he headed for the other side of the room where several bottles stood on a portable bar.

He looked down into Julie's face. "Want one?" he murmured, his voice giving an impression of intimacy, almost purposefully excluding the others.

Wordlessly, she shook her head.

His face assumed a bland expression and he released her hand to quickly and deftly mix whiskey and water. Turning and gently urging Julie in front of him, he guided them to the unoccupied sofa and seated himself, pulling her down closely alongside him.

He took a large swallow of his drink. "So, you didn't answer me, how was Mexico City?" Reluctantly, his eyes left Julie to issue the casual question to Angela.

Anger glittered dangerously in the look which she gave him. The possessive air he demonstrated toward Julie had not gone unnoticed.

"It was . . ." she paused for effect, "very entertaining. I spent some delightful hours with friends and they very nearly convinced me to remain indefinitely." Keenly she calculated the effect of her words.

"You should have," came the negligent reply. "A few months among well-heeled business connections in Mexico could be very worthwhile."

Her stunned expression was echoed by both Julie and Mrs. Brandt. If Angela had expected Alex to welcome her return with anything more than casual interest, she had certainly been disabused. A flurry of questions churned in Julie's mind as she puzzled over the apparent lack of personal interest in Angela's affairs by Alex.

Two bright spots of color burned in Angela's cheeks as she turned to her hostess.

"If I didn't know Alex so well and so long," she said with a short humorless laugh, "I might think that all he cares about is business." Her hard, bright look met his bland, straight one. "However, I do know you, darling, and you are not at all what you like people to think." And with a vicious look at Julie, and not having addressed one word to her, she picked up her handbag.

"Much as I would love to stay, I must run as I promised to meet a friend for dinner." She pouted playfully, looking at Alex. "My car is in the shop, darling. I wonder if you would drive me home."

Alex rose politely from the sofa.

"Unfortunately, Julie and I are planning to leave in a few moments, Angela. However, let me call a taxi for you."

Without waiting for her consent, Alex walked out of the room leaving behind an uncomfortable silence. For a moment, Julie felt a fleeting sympathy for Angela, whose eyes sparkled angrily at the unsuccessful attempt to commandeer Alex for the few minutes it would have taken to drive her home.

Angela turned abruptly and the bright blue eyes flashed to Julie. "I suppose you think you have the upper hand now that you've wormed your way back into Alex's home," she accused spitefully.

Julie flushed at the unexpectedness of the attack. Dimly, she was aware of a small gasp from her mother-in-law.

"You needn't think Margaret and I are just going to sit back and let you take over now that you've had your little fling." Her voice was thin and she fairly crackled with rage.

After the first shock, Julie slowly rose from the sofa, one part of her registering the attack from Angela with surprise as she had never expected an open declaration, while another was concerned for her mother-in-law who, she suspected, was more appalled by Angela's viciousness than was good for her in her condition. She drew a deep breath, grimly determined not to be riled.

"I'm sure you won't wish to upset Alex's mother, Angela," she stated quietly with a meaningful look at the enraged woman. "Anything you wish to say to me can wait until we are both alone."

"Don't give me that solicitous nonsense," Angela spat. "You know you don't give a flip for Margaret's welfare. All you're interested in is Alex. Well, I can tell you this, you'll never have him again. You had your chance and you were a miserable failure."

Julie felt the surge of pure rage that swept over her at Angela's words. Any attempt at caution disappeared in the primitive urge she had to wound this woman who had openly done everything she could to destroy her marriage.

"You'd like to run me off again, wouldn't you, Angela? Well, you did once, but you won't this time." In the heat consuming her, Julie forgot her intention to leave. She would prefer to stay forever, she thought grimly, just to spite Angela rather than to give her the satisfaction of knowing that her marriage to Alex had failed again.

She directed a scornful look into the face of the woman who represented everything hurtful to her.

"You have had your chance for the past two years. What happened? Couldn't you bring him around?"

Angela whitened and opened her mouth to reply.

"Oh, God, please don't." Mrs. Brandt's whispered plea reached Julie's ears, shocking her into an awareness of the pain which the scene being enacted before her must mean to her mother-in-law.

She ran over to the chair and dropped down to catch the hands which trembled on Mrs. Brandt's lap.

"Oh, Mrs. Brandt, please forgive me. I don't know what came over me. Let me take you to your room."

Quickly, she placed the walker and helped her mother-in-law up, ignoring Angela as she angrily surveyed them.

Alex's appearance in the door went almost unnoticed in the strained atmosphere. His quick, penetrating look encompassed all three. No one spoke.

Under his steady gaze, Julie fumbled awkwardly with the walker, disregarding the puzzled frown on his face, suddenly stern and forbidding.

"Your mother is going to her room, Alex." Not quite meeting his eyes, she began ushering her toward the door. "Why don't you entertain Angela while I help her?" Determinedly, she managed to guide the distressed woman through the door and purposefully continued on to her room.

Once inside, Mrs. Brandt sat down heavily on her bed. Julie was horrified to see tears streaming down the lined and slightly drawn features.

"Please don't be upset, Mrs. Brandt." In her distress, she had picked up the hands which were limp and unresponsive in her lap. She began to chafe them warmly and steadily. "I could bite out my tongue for losing my temper like that. I know it must have upset you. Let me call Sarah to get you some strong hot tea." Moving away, she was stopped by the hands which tugged weakly at her skirt.

"Julie, I hope you don't think I supported anything Angela said just now," she said earnestly. "I don't know how I could have misjudged a person as I have Angela." Her voice trembled as her distress increased. "Angela dropped in unexpectedly. The things she said before you both arrived . . . I couldn't believe what she planned." Almost incoherent, her hands went up to cover her face. "She wanted me to help her break up your marriage again." She raised her eyes to Julie's distressed face. "You know that I would never do anything like that, don't you, Julie?"

Julie removed some tissues from a box nearby and thrust them into her mother-in-law's lap.

"Here now, wipe off those tears and forget about Angela. I know that you would never stoop to anything as spiteful as planning to ruin your own son's marriage. It's ridiculous to even think such a thing." Briskly, she uttered the words calculated to reassure Mrs. Brandt while cursing herself for allowing the whole situation to develop. "Now, I'm going to get Sarah. You just sit there for a minute and try to calm yourself."

Sarah, somehow sensing her presence was needed, appeared in the hall and Julie quickly dispatched her to the kitchen for tea. Alex's large frame loomed in the dimness of the hall.

"What has happened?" he demanded savagely. "What in God's name is going on?"

Suddenly the events of the past hour overwhelmed Julie and with a short gasp, and flinging him an agonized look, she fled.

Chapter Nine

In her room, Julie sank down on the bed, Angela's venomous remarks echoing round and round inside her head. During the attack she had immediately burned with her own anger and urge to retaliate. Then her mother-in-law's obvious distress and need had surmounted any personal reaction which Julie might have felt. Now, however, she weakly succumbed to the hurt and humiliation of the woman's open attack. That Angela had felt confident enough in Alex's home to blatantly state her feelings and openly threaten to oust Alex's own wife was incredible.

The sudden opening of her bedroom door startled Julie and with wide eyes darkened with emotion she faced her husband. In wordless inquiry, he surveyed her. She stood with unconscious dignity, returning his appraisal, her chin imperceptibly lifted.

Alex raked a hand through his black hair, shaking his head. "I've been with my mother," he explained. "I'm not sure I understand exactly what went on when I went to call the taxi but Mother insisted that I apologize to you on her behalf." His gaze traveled over her set face as though seeking some indication of her feelings. "What the hell happened in there, Julie? What did Angela say to you that upset my mother?"

Painfully, Julie acknowledged that Alex's first concern lay with his mother. Once—it seemed so long ago now—his concern had been for her, his wife. The look she gave him revealed nothing. "Why don't you ask her?"

"She's gone! I hustled her into that taxi as fast as I could."

He really sounded convincing, Julie thought cynically. Anyway, he was probably glad to see her go under the circumstances. He could always explain to her later that in order to keep his mother in a tranquil frame of mind, it was necessary to tolerate his wife. Her soft mouth twisted bitterly.

"Well, what happened? I intend to find out if I have to choke it out of you, Julie." There was no mistaking his grim intent as her eyes collided with his stormy dark ones.

"Angela was warning me off you, Alex. It upset your mother because she tried to enlist her help to oust me from this house." Julie watched him as he assimilated her words. The frown on his face deepened.

"I'm sorry your mother is upset. I never intended that to happen. I lost my temper."

His look sharpened. "What do you mean?"

She looked away guiltily. "When she began saying all those things at first I tried to stay calm, to refuse to get into an argument with her." Her eyes returned to his. "But soon I couldn't help myself. I couldn't let her get away with saying those nasty things." Her indignant remark hung in the air between them.

A muscle twitched in Alex's jaw and his mouth moved in amusement.

"Gave her a piece of your mind, huh?"

Julie's head ducked low. "I should have waited. Your mother was terribly upset."

His hands reached out and pulled her gently against him. "If I go back into her room and tell her that we are going out to dinner, just the two of us, very cozy, she will probably assume that everything is fine, that you accept her apology, even though you feel none was needed, and everything will be fine and dandy." She felt his mouth move against her temple, stirring the soft hair, then moving slowly down her cheek. Her heart began to beat rapidly. She mustn't give in to the almost irresistible desire to have him kiss her. She didn't understand Alex. One minute he was a remote stranger and the next he was making teasing, gentle love to her. Until she learned just exactly what his true feelings were, she must resist his magnetic appeal.

Reluctantly, she pulled away from his disturbing closeness, noting wryly the sharp disappointment that she would be denied his kiss. It really was practically impossible to resist Alex, she thought longingly.

"Alright, let's go out for dinner." She turned away as she tried to compose her voice and face, unwilling for him to know the havoc he could cause with so little effort.

She felt his silent regard but refused to turn.

"Can you be ready in about thirty minutes?" No traceable emotion could be heard in his voice.

"Sure. I'll be ready." Squaring her shoulders, she

walked to the bathroom and once inside firmly closed the door.

The extra time Julie spent on her makeup and dress that evening were not wasted, if the look in Alex's eyes was anything to judge by, Julie thought with conflicting emotions. His thorough assessment brought a faint pink into her cheeks in spite of her determined effort to remain indifferent. How skillfully he played the part of the admiring husband, she thought cynically. With an effort she forced her thoughts away from the inevitable tendency to dwell on Alex, reminding herself of her avowed intention to play the sophisticate. A little tardily she acknowledged that it was impossible to control her silly tendency to react when Alex determined to make her do so. Alex had always considered it a most endearing trait, this lack of self-possession when he openly demonstrated his desire for her as he had done so often during the early months of their marriage. But she must not think of that.

He moved nearer to her, his male beauty enhanced by the evening clothes he effortlessly wore. Reluctantly, Julie acknowledged the effect on her heightened senses caused by the blatant sexuality exuded by her husband. Somehow the suit, a navy blue blazer and matching slacks, looked special on his lean frame. Worn with a shirt with tiny tucks down the front, the blazer was casually open, and her eyes flicked over the broad chest nervously, averting quickly to deny the visual appeal his handsome darkness created.

Scolding herself inwardly for the familiar and automatic response to Alex, Julie busied herself in a hurried scramble to locate the handbag which had been left in the room earlier.

"Are you looking for this?" Alex drawled, not bothering to disguise his amusement as he surveyed her flushed features.

She took the proffered bag and began to transfer the contents into the beaded one which matched her outfit.

"You look good enough to eat." She felt his breath stir the hair at her nape and her pulse quickened.

Slipping hastily sideways, she escaped from the magnetic field which surrounded him and drew her inexorably. "I'm ready if you are, Alex," she said breathlessly, willing him to accept her unspoken plea to cease tantalizing her senses. It was all a game to him, an amusing way to exercise his undoubted expertise and, worst of all, to demonstrate how easily he wielded the power over her that he possessed.

Alex sighed and, with an exaggerated shrug, set the glass he was holding on the drinks tray. "I guess that means you won't take time for a drink," he said regretfully, his eyes still laughing at her, although his mouth remained resolutely solemn.

"I don't think I should," came the prim reply. "I haven't had any dinner and on an empty stomach something alcoholic would probably go straight to my head." Firmly she turned toward the door and pointedly waited for him, her whole manner stating her impatience to be off.

"Yes ma'am. Right away." He reached down with a flourish to open the door for them to leave. Leaning over to reach the door handle, he turned his head quickly toward her unsuspecting face and kissed her mouth firmly, his touch so brief that she stood mutely accepting. When he pulled back, only an inch separated their lips and he stared into her eyes.

"You really are adorable, my honey girl," he whispered.

Julie found herself ushered out the door and into the car almost before she had a chance to react. The trip was made with little conversation between the two and it suited Julie to remain silent. Her emotions would definitely not bear close examination and for tonight, she was determined not to try.

The restaurant was located north of Boston on the rocky Atlantic shore. The dining area overlooked the incessant breaking of white-capped waves on fierce, time-worn rocks. The sight was fascinating and Julie found herself again and again gazing out to sea, the turbulent water a fit accompaniment for her frame of mind.

Inside, huge crates of drooping Boston fern hung from ceiling rafters, creating a curiously tranquil contrast to the elements raging outside. Candlelight softened the images of the people around them, rendering anonymous the identities of all but the sensual man opposite her. Julie wondered at the range of delicacies offered and chose lobster in a little spurt of defiance of the gods. If she was to enjoy a special meal with Alex, then let it be. Why not pretend for the moment that they were an ordinary married couple out for a special dinner at a special restaurant—even for a special occasion, she thought defiantly.

Alex refilled her wineglass. Solicitously, he entertained her, tending her needs, inquiring as to her choices. He put himself out to make the evening a memorable one. Her heart sank at the thought that this was a farewell evening and that soon she would no longer have such occasions to enjoy Alex's company. For tonight Alex was good company. They had talked companionably, avoiding any subjects which might intrude on the fragile truce or inject a harsh note. With both their tempers mellowed with good food and wine, they seemed wrapped in a glow and Julie felt a passionate wish that this rare empathy and rapport with Alex would never end.

Deep in her own thoughts, Julie was only vaguely aware of Alex signalling for their check and paying it, exchanging smiling pleasantries with the attentive waiter. When he returned with change on a small tray, Alex's eyes sought hers.

"They have a small dance floor upstairs here. Would you like to try it out?"

Her heartbeat accelerated at the thought of being in Alex's arms, swaying softly to music. Dancing had been one pastime they had both enjoyed and together they made a faultless pair. The wistful look on her face must have been apparent because Alex laughed softly.

"Tempted, aren't you?" he teased.

She dimpled and met his look, lashes veiling her golden eyes.

"Yes, I am. It has been a long time since I was on a dance floor."

He seemed puzzled by her answer. He tipped his head sideways, his gaze exploring her face intently. "What manner of entertainment have you enjoyed for the past two years?"

She colored faintly, strangely reluctant to let him know that her life had been singularly dull without him.

"Occasionally I went to the theater and, of course, I managed to have dinner out fairly often." Let him make of that what he pleased, she thought waspishly. She didn't want him to think she had missed his company and the things they had enjoyed together. A tiny voice in the back of her mind insisted that that was exactly what had happened. That without Alex her life had been boring beyond belief. Throwing herself into her job had served as an antidote to the pain and loss of their separation. But even before Alex reappeared in her life, she had begun to feel restless and dissatisfied.

"Courtney probably managed to keep you entertained," Alex stated flatly and placing a cigarette in his mouth, he snapped the lighter. His eyes, glittering with a fierce anger, met hers through the haze of smoke.

"What do you mean by that?" she demanded, her temper flaring as easily as his own.

"What do you think I mean? I can't imagine you going alone to the theater or anywhere else."

"You seem to have a very vivid imagination," Julie retorted, "and I'm just about ready to leave, Alex. As for dancing, just forget it." She leaned over and lifted her evening bag and stole which were resting on one unused chair and scraped her chair back to stand up. "I should have known I couldn't spend an evening with you without it ending in an argument."

Alex's hand shot out and grasped her wrist, preventing her from standing. "Julie, wait just a minute." His face a mixture of conflicting emotions, Alex paused uncertainly. Julie watched him silently as he sought for words.

"Look," he began hesitantly, "I'm sorry for that

crack about Robert Courtney. It just kind of slipped out before I could control it." He laughed shortly without humor. "I get a bit paranoid on that subject but I won't bring it up again. I promise." He looked steadily into her eyes, searching them intently as though seeking some unspoken message.

Julie sighed deeply, looking away from his straight gaze. "Why did you bring me here tonight, Alex?" She continued to stare sightlessly out of the wide window, lost to the savage beauty framed there.

"I wanted another chance to tell you that I had nothing to do with Angela calling me last night or coming over for a visit today. It was just as much a surprise to me as it was to you." He released his grip on her wrist and slid his hand lower to clasp her fingers warmly. The insidious warmth radiated up her arm and Julie swallowed with difficulty, hoping to disguise the rush of feeling triggered by the sensuous feel of his hand. She knew the flutter of her pulse was evident at her throat and when she turned her gaze to Alex, he was staring at it as though mesmerized.

"Let's go upstairs and dance," he coaxed.

Impotently, she stared at his face, her eyes touching every lean feature. Without another word, she got up and allowed him to lead her to the stairs.

They entered the darkly seductive area where a small live band played softly. A hostess showed them to a tiny table with barely room for the short candle placed on top of it and they sank into the two chairs placed alongside it.

"Do you want a gin and tonic?" Alex inquired when their orders were requested.

"That's fine," Julie murmured, still nervously

wondering whether she had made a dangerous error in accompanying Alex.

"Let's not wait for our drinks," he was saying. "I want to dance with you." He rose and, clasping her hand, pulled her up. They moved toward the dance floor and Alex turned to face her and reached out his arms.

Julie moved into them and sighed deeply. It was so right to be here. Alex placed one of his hands on her waist and took her right hand and lifted it up around his neck. Then his other hand went to her waist so that they were as close together as he intended. Deliberately, Julie refused to think. She gave herself up to the music and the compelling closeness of her husband. They moved effortlessly and fluidly together, dancing as one, as perfectly in tune as the music to which they moved.

Neither spoke but Julie knew that Alex was affected by her nearness. She felt the heat of his body through his clothes and his skin was damp as he touched his chin to her temple. His lips moved in her hair and his arms tightened as he enfolded her ever closer.

When the song ended, a moment passed before Julie realized that it was over. With an effort, she withdrew from Alex's arms and stood for a moment to get her bearings. Then he guided her toward their table where the drinks had arrived. They sat down without speaking and Alex tossed off half his whiskey in the first mouthful. Julie found her hand shaking as she hastily drank from the glass and put it down on the table carefully, conscious of Alex's eyes watching, his expression enigmatic.

"We still do that pretty well together, don't we?" he asked at last, breaking the heavy silence.

Julie nodded her head, unable to speak normally and determined to conceal it from Alex.

"We did lots of things well together, Julie," he persisted, his voice deeply intense. Their eyes were locked and, at the sound of their names, both turned confused and reluctant faces to the familiar one smiling down at them delightedly.

"Alex and Julie! I didn't expect to see you two here." Alight with pleasure, Robert Courtney's open features beamed down on them in the dim atmosphere. "It's really great to meet up with you both." He extended a hand to Alex who was rising slowly, his face grim and closed. Briefly they clasped hands. With a quick glance at her husband, Julie's heart sank at the unkind fate that brought Robert Courtney, of all people, to this place on this particular night.

Robert was turning to Julie. "You are looking as beautiful as ever, Julie," he said warmly, his brown eyes running appreciatively over her.

She gave him a genuine smile. "Thanks, Robert. You look pretty fit yourself."

He laughed and shook his head. "It's the tan. Only skin deep, you know."

She looked surprised. "Oh, have you been traveling south?"

Alex's disbelieving snort evoked startled glances from both Robert and Julie. Julie threw him an outraged look which he met blandly. She turned back to Robert.

"Will you join us for a drink, Robert?" She felt Alex stiffen at the invitation.

"I can't, thanks anyway. I'm entertaining a couple of clients." He gestured toward the corner of the room at a table with several people clustered around it laughing and talking with every evidence of having a fine time. He threw them an amused look. "They are feeling no pain about now and I feel responsible for seeing them safely back to their hotel." He smiled at both Julie and Alex. "Don't keep standing, Alex. I'll just drag this chair up for a minute." He leaned over and pulled up a chair.

Alex silently reseated himself. Julie licked her lips nervously sensing his tension and wishing herself anywhere except where she was.

"So how have you two been?" Robert asked, observing the two of them fondly. "I don't think I've seen you for months and months." He raised his eyebrows inquiringly, his face open and friendly.

It was obvious Alex was not going to reply and Julie began to seethe.

"We've been around, Robert, very busy with our jobs and all that." She sounded like a perfect idiot, Julie thought resentfully. But she had no intention of snubbing Robert and she didn't care what Alex made of it either. Flashing Robert a dazzling smile, she continued. "Are you still attending the theater as often as ever? I've missed the last couple of first nights but I intend to remedy that for the next one." She darted a wicked look at her husband whose scowl was deepening ominously.

"Actually, I've been in Florida trying to finalize a deal there, hence the tan." He grinned whitely. "So I have been a little out of the social whirl myself."

Alex's quiet tones fell into the little silence following. "When were you in Florida?" Steadily he observed Robert.

"I spent most of this winter there. Got the best of both worlds, you might say. Winter in Florida and summer in Boston." His friendly countenance turned back to Julie, softening as he considered her.

"You're looking wonderful, Julie. I'm delighted to see you both tonight. We'll have to get together and make a first night opening." His smile included them both. "I'll give you a ring."

Alex's mouth thinned. "You do that."

A quick frown passed over Robert's face as he considered Alex's remark and his eyes slowly moved to Julie sitting tensely poised, willing the conversation to end.

She forced a smile. "We'll look forward to that, Robert. Nice seeing you," she said as he shoved back his chair and began to thread his way among the tables to rejoin his friends.

The silence that descended when Robert left was heavy and strained.

"Let's get out of here." Alex ground out the words as he rose to his feet.

Wordlessly, Julie gathered her evening bag and stole. She breathed deep and even to control the pent-up anger until they could get to the car.

In a red haze the bill was paid and she stiffly walked alongside Alex in the parking lot. When he would have placed his hand under her elbow at the curb, she jerked away, disdaining any physical reminder of his presence. How dare he treat Robert to such a display of rudeness.

They arrived at the car and Alex unlocked the passenger door. Julie wedged herself in and he slammed the door almost before she was clear of it. Once on his side, he jerked open that door and flung himself into the seat, started the car, and shoved it into gear. Savagely, he backed out and with a squeal of tires, shot out into the street.

In the heat of her anger, Julie could spare no time for fright at his driving. She opened her mouth to speak.

"Don't say it," came the curtly grim command. "If you open your mouth to defend Courtney, I won't be responsible for what I do."

Slightly taken aback by the barely controlled violence leashed behind his words, Julie subsided into silence, the effort to contain the heat in her brain resulting from righteous rage practically choking her.

Alex whipped the powerful car into the driveway with a force that threw her against the door. Flinging him an accusatory look, her tawny eyes sparkling with golden light, she yanked open the door, got out, and slammed it shut. Alex, too, wasted no time vacating the car and when Julie rounded the front end of the car, his hand enclosed her upper arm in a vise grip.

"Let me go, you big beast!" she shouted, beyond controlling the tone of her voice.

"You little fool." Alex's quieter tone was no less intense than her own. "Do you want the whole neighborhood to witness our obvious incompatibility?" His mouth thinned and his eyes challenged hers fiercely. "Don't be concerned that you may not get to say everything you're thinking, little one, because we're going to have it out once and for all just as soon as we get inside behind closed doors."

A little shiver danced down Julie's spine at the warning issued by Alex. Or was it a promise? Suddenly, Julie feared entering the house with Alex while that implacable look tautened his face. The easy, teasing facade which he had presented since he had brought her to his home to play out this charade had disappeared and in its place was a deadly, determined, completely frightening stranger.

Unable to shake off the hard fingers clamped on her arm and strangely unwilling to challenge him verbally again, Julie allowed herself to be marched up to the front door. While Alex leaned around her to open it, she darted a quick look at his face, fierce and darkly foreboding to her warily curious eyes. Quickly she dropped her gaze and trying for a little dignity, offered no further resistance when he ushered her inside.

"Never mind trying to delay the inevitable," Alex said coldly. "What's it to be, your room or mine?"

Julie gasped, the implications of either totally unacceptable.

"Why can't we talk in here?" she demanded, albeit a little less aggressively than before.

Alex ignored her and ruthlessly shoved her down the hall, entering the second door which was his own room.

Seizing the initiative, Julie faced him angrily.

"Why were you so rude to Robert?"

"Why were you so nice to him?"

"I wasn't nice, I mean, I was only being polite!" Flashing her eyes stormily, she gave rein to her inflamed temper fully, glorying in releasing the pent-up emotions which had been seething since their hasty departure from the restaurant. "He's probably wondering if you've taken leave of your senses, or something. At least he knows you have lost your manners."

Rage flared in the silvery eyes. "But he can certainly have no doubt about you. You still find him a fun partner, don't you?" he demanded savagely.

"A fun partner!" Julie gasped indignantly. "What do you mean by that exactly?"

"Don't give me that little innocent outraged act. You spent more time with Robert Courtney than any other person during the time we were married. And that includes your girl friends."

Outraged, Julie glared at him wordlessly. Alex's mouth thinned mockingly. "Do you deny it?"

"If I did, and I'm not agreeing with your preposterous statement, but if I did, it was because I didn't have a husband around to spend time with. You were too busy keeping Angela entertained."

Alex regarded her, an unreadable look on his face, his anger contained momentarily.

"Angela was a business associate only. There was nothing personal there." His reply was delivered flatly as he subjected her to an aloof appraisal.

"Ha! Even your mother wanted Angela to be Mrs. Alex Brandt and don't you dare deny that!" Julie's mouth quivered tremulously. The remembered pain of her mother-in-law's treatment still smarted.

"My mother's choice of a wife for me was completely immaterial to me."

"How can you say such a thing?" Julie's voice rose incredulously. "Her opinion is so immaterial that you went to ridiculous lengths to bring me back just to keep her happy." Turning her back abruptly, Julie stalked over to the dresser and grabbed the masculine-looking brush and began brushing her hair agitatedly.

"You think the attempt to make our marriage work again is ridiculous?" Alex's voice sounded right behind her. She flashed her eyes to his in the mirror.

"Well, don't you? That's hardly a lasting founda-

tion to build on . . . my mother-in-law's health. It
would be nice to have somebody care about me that
much." She flung down the brush with a harsh
clatter.

"You think I don't care about you?" He grasped
her arms tightly, his grip biting into the soft flesh of
her upper arms.

Julie hunched her shoulders trying to escape.

"I wish to hell I didn't care about you!" The
tortured words were wrenched from him and he
released her arms, thrusting his hands through his
hair in an impatient, frustrated gesture.

Julie's eyes filled with tears and she swallowed
trying to prevent them from spilling down her face.

"Spare me the tears!" Impotent fury contorted his
features as he savagely rammed his fists into his
pockets as though confining them before they could
wreak some appalling damage on her.

Her golden eyes flashed. "I'm never going to cry
over you again as long as I live, Alex Brandt! And,"
dashing the tears with the fingers of both hands,
"I'm not going to live with you another minute
either!" Wildly, she looked around seeking a way
around him to escape.

Anticipating her intention, Alex stepped closer. "I
told you we were having this out once and for all
tonight and you're not going to run away again if I
have to hold you here with force." He reached for
her.

"We'll just see about that!" Pivoting sharply
around him, she made a dash for the door. Alex
easily reached her before she had hardly begun. She
looked up into his face, prepared to demand that he
turn her loose and was shocked at the blatant desire
and anger mingled there.

Checked momentarily, her confused brain whirled as she tried to assimilate the evidence of her own eyes. Any further objection to Alex's high-handed tactics would meet with the same treatment. Willing herself to remain calm and not allowing him any advantage if possible, she ceased struggling. Alex kicked the door closed and released her arm, flinging it away as though the touch of her was suddenly offensive.

She placed both hands on her upper arms and began a rather agitated rubbing up and down as she warily regarded the grim stranger facing her. Determined that he not suspect the uncertainty which filled her brain, she tilted her chin.

"Alright, Alex. Here we are in your bedroom through no choice of mine. What next?" Defiantly, she hurled the sarcastic challenge, bravado and fear equally mixed in her bright eyes and tremulous mouth.

"I'll show you what's next!" He reached out and grabbed her shoulders, startling her. Her hands flew against his chest to prevent further contact, but his superior strength merely crushed them against his chest.

"You think you can meet up with your former boyfriend and flirt with him, playing us off against each other and escape without any consequences, don't you?" He bit out the words, his face so close to hers that his breath fanned her face while his eyes, darkened and dilated, surveyed her own amber ones. Then his gaze lowered to her mouth, slightly parted in shock and dawning wonder. Sensually, Alex examined every feature, his anger evident even as Julie sensed an inner conflict. She felt him tremble with emotion. Just how she knew of the ambivalent torment within him, Julie could not explain, but she did know. And with that knowledge, courage and confidence returned.

Alex sensed the change. Narrowly, he focused his eyes on hers and they stared at each other. The tense grip on her shoulders eased imperceptibly.

"You are going to drive me crazy, do you know that?" His tormented words breathed into her mouth, intoxicating her. She waited breathlessly, her lips still parted. With a groan, his head descended. A wild delight possessed her at the first touch of his mouth, gentle, almost reluctantly moving over her lips, back and forth, and then fiercely, frantically, he devoured her mouth, his kiss demanding and receiving her eager response. Julie was dizzy with the pleasure Alex was giving her and she tumbled headlong, spiralling into a whirling space where Alex's mouth and touch were everything.

With a sigh, she lifted her arms around his neck and of its own volition her body strained to fit into the hard contours of his. Eagerly they savored the feel and taste of long forbidden fruit, irresistible and sweet.

He whispered her name over and over and Julie whimpered in pleasure. She felt the rasp of her zipper as he loosened it and slipped the tiny straps off her shoulders. The dress fell onto the floor making a little pool of midnight blue at her feet. Alex's breathing was deep and uncontrolled now as the silken curves of her body surged under his caress. He released the front catch of her bra and feverishly his mouth descended to taste the swelling peaks. His hands were roaming freely, their warmth creating delicious tremors as they surely found each pleasure point, expertly delighting her drugged senses.

Briefly drawing back, seeing the golden glaze of her eyes, Alex's breath drew in sharply. The sight of her face, hectically flushed, features languorous and yielding, served to further ignite his own desperate need, and hungrily he claimed her mouth once more, sensually exploring its contours, ravishing the sweetness within. Julie was trembling and pliant in the circle of his arms, totally without resistance as the conflagration created by their mutual desire threatened to consume them.

"Julie, Julie," his mouth at her ear whispered huskily. "I want to love you again."

Weakly, Julie made an effort to cling to sanity. She knew that in one moment, just a mere fraction of time, there would be no way to resist the ultimate conclusion to the terrifying need which surged between them both. Fleetingly, she considered denying the agonizingly sweet fulfillment which would be hers if she made no effort to object.

Alex picked her up and turned to the bed. In that moment, Julie gave herself up to the magic of the need clamoring within her. With a little moan, she turned her face to Alex's and met his descending mouth.

Chapter Ten

When Julie opened her eyes, she lay confused, momentarily suspended between waking and sleeping. Sunlight filtered through the slight parting of the drapes at the window and she gazed at the bright ray slanting into the room. Suddenly full awareness jolted her awake and turning breathlessly, she viewed the empty pillow. Evidence of Alex's muscled length was shown in the wrinkled covers close beside her and although there was no sound, she wondered if he was already showering in the bathroom.

Reluctantly, she considered the events of last night. Her senses stirred as she remembered. Alex had been the perfect lover, arousing her skillfully and with sensuous expertise until his control had seemed to snap and suddenly he was urgently demanding, a man long deprived, his hands and mouth eagerly searching, finding all the secret places which so long had lain cold and untouched. In a wild frenzy of desire for him, Julie had trembled with anticipation and at last they entered that soaring, flying plane where time diminished, place and space disappeared, and only pleasure and delight were real. Later, caressing her with his warm mouth, Alex had soothed her into the sleep of satiation.

As Julie lay, pensive and considering her position, her thoughts touched tentatively on the one unassailable fact. There could be no doubt that what happened had been unavoidable and, in a sense, necessary after the close proximity of the past few weeks. Evidently, Alex still felt some of the desire for her which had burned so fiercely when first they had loved. It was only natural that, with memories of past intimacy and the undeniable chemistry between them, their coming together had been inevitable. For Julie, it had been the culmination of all her longing and hunger for the only man she would ever love. As for Alex, Julie sighed and a sharp pang tightened her stomach. She was still no closer to discovering Alex's feelings than before.

Pushing aside the sheet which was her only covering, Julie eased out of bed, her toes meeting the plushness of blue carpet. More than normally aware of the sensuous pile under her feet, she stretched luxuriously like a well-fed cat and made her way to the bathroom. It was empty.

Disappointment welled within her but resolutely she pushed away the temptation to indulge in any imagined implication in Alex's absence. After all, no commitment had been made last night and, Julie reminded herself, she was a fully grown adult, not some silly teenager who had been taken advantage of by an unprincipled cad.

Biting her lower lip which trembled in spite of fierce and determined effort, Julie quickly turned on the shower tap and stepped under the stinging spray. Timeless moments passed while she purposely kept her mind blank. With a downbent head, Julie gazed while the water circled and curled around the shiny fixture covering it. Then, methodically, she reached around and turned off the tap, stepped out of the shower, and unfolded a thick towel.

There was no further reason for lying to herself. No more need to keep up the pretense that had been the real reason for her agreeing to return to Alex's home. She still loved Alex, she always would. She could not live with him under the conditions originally laid out by him, and there could be no denying she was still terribly vulnerable as far as he was concerned. He could devastate her just by being himself. It was not his fault, she knew now. It was nobody's fault.

Therefore, she would have to get out and right away. A repeat of last night she could not bear. For Alex to casually possess her when the mood was upon him would be soul-destroying to her if she allowed it to happen. For him to desire her was not enough. She would have his love or nothing. Fleetingly, last night she had pretended that the tumultuous passion and undoubted sexual compatibility might be enough to satisfy her longing for a satisfying relationship with Alex. But in the cold light of morning, her body still tender and satiated from his lovemaking, Julie knew with an anguish awful in its intensity, that she wanted more than that. She wanted Alex to delight in her company and to burn with impatience to see her at the end of each and every day. She wanted to be the woman he liked, not only loved, best in all the world. She could not settle for less.

Swallowing past the lump in her throat with difficulty, Julie braced to meet Alex, who must be up and about already. Poised by the open door, she cast a last look around the room. It was firmly stamped with Alex's personality. In the heat of the moment when Alex had marched her into his room last night, no details had made any impression. And during the time she had been back in his home, she had resolutely avoided this particular room. Now she gazed about her curiously, almost impersonally. She was fully aware that the room, which was the master bedroom and had been shared by them when first married, was almost completely unchanged. The furnishings were just as she had placed them, draperies and accessories the same. Alex had made no effort to erase memories of their occupation of the room. Quietly she slipped out of the room.

Sarah met her almost immediately, her homely features strained and anxious.

"Oh, Miss Julie, I was just going to come in and wake you. Mr. Alex had to rush out a few minutes ago to take Mrs. Brandt to the hospital."

"What happened, Sarah?" Another stroke, the thought flashed across her startled brain. Another could kill her.

The elderly maid was wringing her hands agitatedly as she explained. "She was going to make herself an early morning cup of coffee and somehow Mrs. Brandt's arm was scalded with boiling water."

Relief caused Julie's tightly held breath to release in a strong rush and she weakly leaned against the wall, resting there until the strength returned to her rubbery legs. It was not a stroke after all. During the weeks she had spent living in this house, Julie had learned to appreciate the qualities which her mother-in-law did possess. True, she was a strong-willed woman, but that characteristic also lent itself to a strong determination to right the wrong done to her daughter-in-law. She had handsomely set out to make Julie's second stay in this house a happy one and had made her as welcome as it was possible for her to do. If his mother sometimes suspected Alex showed less openness and affection to Julie than he had done formerly, she never mentioned it. Neither did she level any subtle accusations toward Julie for her puzzling lack of response as a bride might do in a storybook reconciliation with her lover.

Sighing deeply, Julie brought her mind back to the immediate problem. Although she sincerely regretted Mrs. Brandt's accident, it was not something which would require her to remain in the house. Therefore, her plan to leave would be possible after all and the sooner the better. Since Alex would be tied up at the emergency ward in the hospital with his mother, it seemed the perfect time to leave.

Becoming aware of Sarah's anxious gaze and that the elderly woman was still awaiting some response, Julie forced a smile which she hoped seemed halfway normal.

"You frightened me for a moment, Sarah. I was afraid Mrs. Brandt might have had another stroke. Thank goodness it wasn't that." Julie's hand nervously swept her tawny hair away from her face as she turned back to walk on down the hall.

"Don't you want any breakfast, Miss Julie?"

"Not right now, thanks, Sarah. I think I'll just skip it this morning. I've a few things to take care of in my room." She passed the door of the master bedroom averting her eyes hastily and entered her own room, softly closing the door behind her.

Quickly, she pulled out two matching pieces of luggage and packed most of her personal items raked from the top of her dresser. Other drawers contained sweaters and tops which she transferred to the case. Then she moved to the closet and seeing that there would not be room for everything, she selected several outfits to see her through the next few days and placed them inside the second case. Shoes and other accessories were added and she closed the cases, lifted them from the bed, and carried them to the door.

Once everything was transferred to the front door, Julie surveyed the items and knew that it would take more than one trip to get them all into her car. The sound of the door must have reached Sarah, for she appeared, her eyes widened in surprise as she surveyed the luggage and other articles stacked at Julie's feet.

"Miss Julie! What are you doing? Where are you going?" Surprise and concern raised her voice.

Julie sighed resignedly. Some explanation would have to be made; otherwise it would not be beyond Sarah to give Alex a hysterical call at the emergency ward of the hospital. That must be avoided at all costs.

"Sarah, I know you won't understand this, but I must leave the house for a while."

She had barely begun when Sarah interrupted.

"But does Mr. Alex know?"

Frustration sharpened Julie's tone. "Not really, Sarah, but that doesn't matter. I . . ."

"Oh, Miss Julie, you can't leave like that again. Please wait until Mr. Alex gets back." Wringing both hands in agitation, she appealed to Julie, whose urge to leave was greater than ever.

Taking refuge in coolness and subtly stressing her role as mistress, although second in command, she thought almost hysterically, she gave Sarah what she hoped was an unforthcoming look.

"Please tell Alex that I will be in touch, Sarah, and

I must go now." Picking up two cases, she stepped through the door and went out to her car.

Soon her things were transferred to the car and she was on her way, relief and unhappiness warring within her. Tears blurred her vision and she kept raking her hands over her streaming eyes, but it was a futile effort. Finally, she pulled over to the side of the street and just wept. After a few minutes, she managed to control the tears enough to drive, so she pulled back into the stream of traffic, furtively looking around to see if anyone had noticed her pathetic little display. Absolute indifference characterized the people within cars as well as those outside on the streets. A little chagrined and hiccupping now and then, Julie drove on.

Julie pulled in at the curb in front of her apartment and after locking her car, climbed the steps whose familiarity provoked no feeling. Dispirited and weary, she reached for the old-fashioned doorknob and pushed it open. Trudging through the vestibule and down the hall, she entered her own silent apartment.

She jumped when an hour later the doorbell rang, startled out of her miserable thoughts at the harsh sound.

With no preliminaries, Alex's voice carried into the room. "I came for you, Julie. I know you're here because your car is outside."

Julie rose from the sofa, her knees shaking. All color drained from her face and panic clutched at her heart as she stared at the unmistakable outline of her husband revealed in the tiny space opened by the chain. Alex's face loomed at her, a grim expression chiseled there. That he was obstinately determined to enter and speak to her she knew and any effort on her part to refuse was absolutely futile. Julie released the chain and the door swung forward violently from the push of strong hands, impatient and angry.

Alex's icy gaze encountered Julie's uncertain one. Preemptorily, he issued the order. "Get your things. We're leaving." Alex reached out and closed his hand around her upper arm, the strong grip leaving her no doubt of his intention.

Julie was suddenly overwhelmed with a sensation of futility and pain. The biting grip of Alex's possession of her arm, their failed attempt to live together again, the fury which threatened to overcome him when he was with her for only a few minutes . . . everything whirled together in a darkened void and Alex's voice receded as a roaring sound drowned out all but the consuming blackness engulfing her. With a wordless whimper, consciousness left her and she folded like a weakened flower against a shocked Alex.

When she came to, Julie opened her eyes and encountered the cool, gray gaze of her husband. She turned away, not able to continue the contest of wills which was necessary in dealing with him. In turning away, she missed the look of pain and self-loathing which tightened his dark features.

"Julie," he began huskily, "you scared me half out of my mind. Do you feel alright now?" Anxiously, he surveyed her white face, his eyes devouring every line of it. When her eyes filled with weak, futile tears, he picked up her hand and carrying it to his mouth, he pressed his lips against it passionately.

"Please don't cry. I know I behaved like an animal coming in here, but I swear to God, I never meant to hurt you." His voice was ragged and low in its intensity. "When you fainted right at my feet, it scared the hell out of me. I don't know why I keep on upsetting you. Believe me, that's not what I intend."

Through her tears, Julie managed a small smile. "I guess it's just not meant for us to deal together peaceably, Alex. All we do is cause each other pain and irritation." *Pain for me and irritation for you,* Julie qualified silently as she regarded Alex. Naturally, he was sorry to have precipitated this ridiculous happening. No one could be unmoved when a person passes out at their feet but there was no need for her to place any further construction on Alex's words. She drew a deep breath.

"I think I can get up now, Alex. I don't know why I fainted, but it's over now and I'll be perfectly alright after I have something to eat. As a matter of fact, I skipped breakfast and it's past time for lunch." Refusing to meet his steady gaze, Julie eased into an upright position. A slight dizzy sensation remained, but it cleared immediately and she felt able to face Alex. Tugging her hand free, she eased away from his compelling nearness, damping down the almost irresistible desire to lean weakly against him and feel the comforting strength of his strong arms enfold her in tenderness and love rather than anger and bitterness.

"I know you came here to talk, Alex," she began haltingly, "but if you don't mind, I'd like to put it off a couple of days, until I've had a chance to settle back into my apartment and everything could get back to normal for both of us."

"Normal!" he exploded. "What do you know about normal? For the past two years we have lived a most abnormal existence. And I intend to see that we change all that." Exasperation threaded his words as he fixed her with a look of impatience and barely contained fury. When Julie warily leaned away, he seemed to realize that he was beginning to overwhelm her again and he drew a long breath, pausing patiently to resume once more in gentler tones.

"Look, Julie. Let's try to consider the situation without getting all riled up, hmm?"

Julie resolutely hardened herself against his charm. "I'm not riled up, Alex. I just said that I would like to get settled in my apartment again. Don't you think that would be best all around?"

"Hell, no! I want you back at home where you belong." He threw her a puzzled look. "Didn't last night mean anything to you? Can we share something like that and you just get up the next morning and calmly walk out without a word?"

Julie inhaled sharply, the pain of what he was saying thrusting unmercifully into her already lacerated feelings.

"That's really unfair, Alex. What did you expect me to do after last night? Do you want to install me in your house and have me at your beck and call anytime of the night or day . . . that is, when you happen to be home," she added sarcastically. "Then when you tire of me, just send me back to my apartment. I suppose you thought I would just resume my life as before when you did release me, as I had managed to put together some kind of existence for two years without you? Is that what you have in mind?" she demanded angrily.

"Are you crazy? That's about the most stupid thing you have ever come up with, Julie. I'll never get tired of you. I never did get tired of you, although you certainly didn't prove to have much staying power the first time around, I might add." The bitter ring of his words echoed hollowly as Julie sat stunned. The silence after Alex's words stretched unnoticed as she considered the incredible statement that he never had tired of her.

"I brought you back because I couldn't stand to live without you any longer," he stated quietly. "No woman could satisfy my need for a beautiful, honey blond who drives me to distraction, but who is the only woman in the world for me."

"Oh, Alex," Julie breathed in astonishment, her eyes bright and incredulous as they gazed at him with all her love and longing openly revealed.

He reached for her and folded his arms around her, crushing her against his chest and burying his face in the tawny hair. Julie's hands went around his neck and lovingly caressed the back of his head, the feel of his skin and hair wondrously satisfying as she threaded her fingers through it and turned her mouth against his strong throat, inflaming her senses with the fragrance of his masculinity.

"Why did you leave me this morning?" he demanded thickly, his lips touching her face lightly at her cheeks and temples and brows.

Shyly, she lowered her lashes, the sight of his face shining with love overwhelming her. "When I woke and you weren't there, I tried not to think about how you had not said you loved me, how you had made no commitment once again. I didn't know your feelings and I suddenly knew that I could not live with you without your love. I wanted it more than anything in the world," she ended tremulously.

He kissed her gently. "I didn't realize you needed to actually hear the words. Every kiss and every touch last night was intended to show my love. You've always had my love, even when we were apart. I knew there could never be anyone I could love as I loved you."

"Why did you let me go, Alex?" she asked, the remembered pain of separation darkening her eyes.

He drew in a deep breath. "At first, when you failed to return after the snowstorm, I was mad with jealousy and rage. I could have killed you for putting me through such torture." His gaze focused on a faraway scene. He shook his head as if to clear an unpleasant memory. "When you did return, I was too angry to be reasonable. To be honest, I wasn't really aware of the depth of my love and need for you. I stupidly thought that it would be best if we did separate. You'll have to admit, those last few months weren't very enjoyable."

As if recalling that time conjured up memories which he would rather forget, Alex loosened his hold on Julie and reached into his pocket for his cigarettes. He shook one out and lighted it, frowning through the haze of smoke which enveloped them momentarily.

"It didn't take long for me to realize that I had made a big mistake in letting you go." He laughed ruefully. "When you got back after being marooned with Robert Courtney during the storm, I couldn't tolerate the thought of him possessing you." He slanted a glance toward her face, his mouth pulled wryly. "I couldn't imagine that any man could spend two days with you and manage to resist your charms, either."

Julie leaned over and stroked her hand down his lean cheek. "Robert was never anything but a sympathetic friend. Somehow he sensed right away the situation which existed between your mother and me and I desperately needed some moral support from someone who understood and sympathized. That's all it ever was."

Alex reached out and violently crushed his cigarette. Then pushing aside the ash tray, he turned to Julie. "And, of course, after the terrible row we had, when I had cooled down, I thought I had pushed you into Robert's arms. I thought you had gone to him." His eyes mirrored the anguish of that time, dark, slate gray, the pain he must have suffered clearly revealed to her for the first time.

"My mother's stroke came at the worst possible time," he said in a low voice. "I was suddenly in a position where I was in constant attendance at the hospital with her and, since she was so completely dependent on me, I felt I couldn't desert her." He frowned in remembrance. "I was made unpleasantly aware that my mother's attitude toward me was one of unhealthy possessiveness. It occurred to me then that she may have gone to quite desperate lengths to remove any supposed threat to the status quo." The look he turned on Julie was compounded of guilt and regret. "I was forced to face up to the fact that you may have been driven away from me by circumstances that I should have been on guard to prevent. You can't imagine my feelings during that time."

Julie's quick, sympathetic murmur drew a negative shake of his raven black head. "No, I don't deserve your generous heart to forgive me that easily, darling. I was punished alright." He laughed shortly. "I was forced to attend my mother while tortured with thoughts of you free of the restraints of a marriage which could not possibly have brought you anything but pain and unhappiness. I simply had to bide my time, keeping tabs on you as best I could until I could devote all of myself to winning you back and your love. It was hell."

His eyes darkened sensually as he surveyed her distressed face. He pulled her onto his lap, burying his face in her throat, his mouth trailing warm kisses downward, encountering the sweet curve of her breasts.

Julie slid her hands into the opening of his shirt, savoring the crisp feel of the dark hair on his chest against her palms and thrilling when she felt him shudder with pleasure, knowing at last that it was within her power to arouse him as he could so easily arouse her. And that it was because of love.

Minutes later, she placed both hands alongside his face. "Alex, why did you insist on installing me in your house? Did you persuade your mother to go along with your plan?" The thought that her mother-in-law's change of heart might be false was more painful than Julie would have believed a few short weeks ago.

Alex reluctantly allowed her to distract him. Smiling gently, his hands caressing still, he explained. "It was true that after her illness Mother regretted her treatment of you when we first married. She was eager to make amends and," with a rueful twist of his mouth, "I saw it as the perfect excuse to get you to myself on my home grounds. What I hadn't counted on was that you would succeed in holding me off as long as you did."

Julie flushed and buried her face in his chest.

"It wasn't easy. Every time you touched me I went up in flames. I'll never know how I managed to resist . . . except," her brows puckered thoughtfully, "my need to have your love was stronger than my physical need for you."

Alex's hold tightened fiercely. "I'm afraid I wasn't capable of making any such distinctions. I wanted you under any circumstances . . . any way I could get you." His urgent words were punctuated with quick, hard kisses.

Julie's reaction must have been satisfactory, because he relaxed his hold to meet her warm gaze, her golden eyes lingering on each hard, masculine feature. Alex met the look of love with a tenderness in his own eyes, then he laughed suddenly. Seeing her puzzled smile, he explained. "I wanted to live with you alone with no distractions and no people around while we worked out our problems. And, my mother seemed delighted with my idea and even suggested that she would start looking for a smaller place where Sarah could provide domestic help. It couldn't have worked out better."

Julie was quiet as she thought about Alex's efforts to resume their marriage. It seemed incredible that she could have been so unaware of his love. He had gone about repairing their marriage in the way in which he did anything which was important to him, with a singleness of purpose and determination. Alex's behavior was totally in character. The only surprising thing was that she had been unable to see it, to even suspect the lengths to which he was prepared to go.

"I suppose Angela's appearance on the scene came as a surprise, didn't it?" Julie quizzed, darting a sharp glance to gauge his reaction.

Alex's features darkened as he replied, "I could have strangled her cheerfully. I thought everything was beginning to work out. You were responding beautifully. Frank's business was booming." He laughed wryly. "Just shows that a person shouldn't start congratulating himself until all the tricks are in."

Watching him steadily, Julie ventured, "You felt nothing for her by then?"

"I felt nothing for her ever. Our relationship was strictly business. I was pretty firmly involved in a deal with her father and she fancied herself as assisting him and he indulgently allowed her her head in some of his ventures." Alex's brows drew together slightly as he directed a straight look into her eyes. "She may have had some idea that we would get together, and Mother will have to take the responsibility for fostering any hopes she may have had in that direction. But as for me, Angela has always left me cold. She is that, Julie," he said gently, lovingly tender as he considered her flushed face, "she is a cold, calculating woman. I needed someone who was warm and giving. I needed you."

Julie drew a deep, satisfying breath. "I do love you, Alex," she whispered.

"And I adore you, my honey girl." His mouth lowered in sensual possession and Julie's heart swelled with incredible joy.

A few pleasurable minutes passed, the only sounds the quickened breathing and incoherent endearments as they surrendered to the heady delight of rediscovery. Julie stirred after a moment when a thought suddenly occurred and breaking away from Alex's possessive hold, she pushed against his arms to meet his eyes, darkened with the desire which answered his in the depths of her own tawny ones.

"What about your sudden appearance at the office? I suppose that was planned in advance, too?" A laughing frown framed her indignant demand.

He chuckled softly. "Right first time. I heard Peters-Winton was having a rough time and wrangled an invitation to a party which Frank was going to attend. We met informally there and I simply followed up with a letter suggesting that I might be able to ferret out some of the problems in his organization." He grinned at her indignation. "It was a piece of cake and my little wife was just two doors down the hall the whole time."

"Beast!" Julie accused laughingly. "I couldn't decide whether to act indifferent or succumb to my natural inclination to fall into your arms." She shook her head ruefully. "I suppose all along I knew it was just a matter of time before you realized the effect you had on me. It was just as potent as it was the first time I ever saw you."

Alex lowered his head and kissed her with rising ardor. "I don't know what I've done to deserve you, but nothing is ever going to separate us again, Julie. That's a promise."

He raised his hand and gently pushed her tumbled hair away from her face, his gaze lingering on the well-kissed look of her mouth.

"All these weeks when you've been across the table from me at home or sitting with me in the evenings, it has been torture for me to keep my hands off you." His teasing grin flashed. "Didn't you notice I had a lot of paperwork to do in my den?"

Julie's mouth opened as realization dawned.

"I thought you were just avoiding me. Even your mother was puzzled by your neglect since we were supposed to be acting out a big reconciliation."

"There won't be any more acting from this moment on," Alex promised, his voice lowering to a husky growl while his mouth made tantalizing little forays down her neck and into the gentle swell where her blouse was parted invitingly. "As soon as we leave here, we're going home and you're not going to see daylight for about a week."

Julie smiled slowly. "Sounds good to me."

Genuine Silhouette
sterling silver bookmark
for only $15.95!

What a beautiful way to hold your place in your current romance! This genuine sterling silver bookmark, with the distinctive Silhouette symbol in elegant black, measures 1½" long and 1" wide. It makes a beautiful gift for yourself, and for every romantic you know! And, at only $15.95 each, including all postage and handling charges, you'll want to order several now, while supplies last.

Send your name and address with check or money order for $15.95 per bookmark ordered to

Simon & Schuster Enterprises
120 Brighton Rd., P.O. Box 5020
Clifton, N.J. 07012
Attn: Bookmark

Bookmarks can be ordered pre-paid only. No charges will be accepted. Please allow 4-6 weeks for delivery.

N.Y. State Residents
Please Add Sales Tax

Silhouette Romance

IT'S YOUR OWN SPECIAL TIME

Contemporary romances for today's women.
Each month, six very special love stories will be yours
from SILHOUETTE. Look for them wherever books are sold
or order now from the coupon below.

$1.50 each

Hampson	□ 1 □ 4 □ 16 □ 27 □ 28 □ 52 □ 94	Browning	□ 12 □ 38 □ 53 □ 73 □ 93
Stanford	□ 6 □ 25 □ 35 □ 46 □ 58 □ 88	Michaels	□ 15 □ 32 □ 61 □ 87
Hastings	□ 13 □ 26	John	□ 17 □ 34 □ 57 □ 85
Vitek	□ 33 □ 47 □ 84	Beckman	□ 8 □ 37 □ 54 □ 96
Wildman	□ 29 □ 48	Wisdom	□ 49 □ 95
		Halston	□ 62 □ 83

□ 5 Goforth	□ 22 Stephens	□ 50 Scott	□ 81 Roberts
□ 7 Lewis	□ 23 Edwards	□ 55 Ladame	□ 82 Dailey
□ 9 Wilson	□ 24 Healy	□ 56 Trent	□ 86 Adams
□ 10 Caine	□ 30 Dixon	□ 59 Vernon	□ 89 James
□ 11 Vernon	□ 31 Halldorson	□ 60 Hill	□ 90 Major
□ 14 Oliver	□ 36 McKay	□ 63 Brent	□ 92 McKay
□ 19 Thornton	□ 39 Sinclair	□ 71 Ripy	□ 97 Clay
□ 20 Fulford	□ 43 Robb	□ 76 Hardy	□ 98 St. George
□ 21 Richards	□ 45 Carroll	□ 78 Oliver	□ 99 Camp

$1.75 each

Stanford	□ 100 □ 112 □ 131	Browning	□ 113 □ 142 □ 164 □ 172 □ 191
Hardy	□ 101 □ 130 □ 184	Michaels	□ 114 □ 146
Cork	□ 103 □ 148 □ 188	Beckman	□ 124 □ 154 □ 179
Vitek	□ 104 □ 139 □ 157 □ 176	Roberts	□ 127 □ 143 □ 163 □ 180 □ 199
Dailey	□ 106 □ 118 □ 153 □ 177 □ 195	Trent	□ 110 □ 161 □ 193
Bright	□ 107 □ 125	Wisdom	□ 132 □ 166
Hampson	□ 108 □ 119 □ 128 □ 136	Hunter	□ 137 □ 167 □ 198
	□ 147 □ 151 □ 155 □ 160	Scott	□ 117 □ 169 □ 187
	□ 178 □ 185 □ 190 □ 196	Sinclair	□ 123 □ 174
		John	□ 115 □ 192

$1.75 each

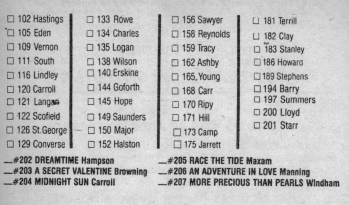

☐ 102 Hastings	☐ 133 Rowe	☐ 156 Sawyer	☐ 181 Terrill
☐ 105 Eden	☐ 134 Charles	☐ 158 Reynolds	☐ 182 Clay
☐ 109 Vernon	☐ 135 Logan	☐ 159 Tracy	☐ 183 Stanley
☐ 111 South	☐ 138 Wilson	☐ 162 Ashby	☐ 186 Howard
☐ 116 Lindley	☐ 140 Erskine	☐ 165, Young	☐ 189 Stephens
☐ 120 Carroll	☐ 144 Goforth	☐ 168 Carr	☐ 194 Barry
☐ 121 Langan	☐ 145 Hope	☐ 170 Ripy	☐ 197 Summers
☐ 122 Scofield	☐ 149 Saunders	☐ 171 Hill	☐ 200 Lloyd
☐ 126 St.George	☐ 150 Major	☐ 173 Camp	☐ 201 Starr
☐ 129 Converse	☐ 152 Halston	☐ 175 Jarrett	

—#202 DREAMTIME Hampson   —#205 RACE THE TIDE Maxam
—#203 A SECRET VALENTINE Browning   —#206 AN ADVENTURE IN LOVE Manning
—#204 MIDNIGHT SUN Carroll   —#207 MORE PRECIOUS THAN PEARLS Windham

$1.95 each

—#208 SUNSET IN PARADISE Halston   —#211 GREEK IDYLL Walters
—#209 TRAIL OF THE UNICORN LaDame   —#212 YESTERDAY'S PROMISE Young
—#210 FLIGHT OF FANCY Eden   —#213 SEPARATE CABINS Dailey

Look for _PRACTICAL DREAMER_ by Dixie Browning
available in May and
WESTERN MAN by Janet Dailey in June.

SILHOUETTE BOOKS, Department SB/1
1230 Avenue of the Americas
New York, NY 10020

Please send me the books I have checked above. I am enclosing
$_____ (please add 50¢ to cover postage and handling. NYS and
NYC residents please add appropriate sales tax). Send check or
money order—no cash or C.O.D.'s please. Allow six weeks for delivery.

NAME_____

ADDRESS_____

CITY_____ STATE/ZIP_____

Silhouette Romance

Coming next month from
Silhouette Romances

Love So Rare by Anne Hampson

Dawn had unwillingly married Ralf Deverell, yet as the weeks passed, she realized she had fallen in love—with a husband who wanted to keep their marriage a secret.

Her Mother's Keeper by Nora Roberts

How could anyone fall for the unscrupulous author Luke Powers? Gwen knew that she should persuade him to return to California, only now, he'd be taking her heart with him!

Love's Sweet Music by Jean Saunders

Accompanying pianist Paul Blake on his Continental tour was a dream come true for Angela Raines. Her only fear: he saw her as another easy conquest.

Blue Mist Of Morning by Donna Vitek

Anne Fairchild made it a rule never to get involved with her boss. However, Ty Manning left her little choice and before she knew it, he was commanding her love.

Fountains Of Paradise by Elizabeth Hunter

Jewelry designer Michal Brent went to Sri Lanka to buy unusual and beautiful stones. But the most precious jewel she found was the jade green glance of Hendrik Van de Aa.

Island Spell by Dorothy Cork

Working for author Guy Desailley on his island retreat was no easy task for Aidan Elliot. The attraction was immediate—but could love blossom when they were both so cynical about romance?